Dan gently tilted Cathy's head up

His mouth brushed over hers gently, exploringly, and she trembled violently, leaning toward him as he finally took full possession of her lips, his kiss deepening with a shock of desire that tensed his whole body.

Cathy moaned as his mouth invaded with sensual expertise, her hands moving blindly to his powerful shoulders, clinging to him.

She had never received such a kiss before, and she was frightened of her own response to it. A shaft of awareness, of pure sexual excitement, pierced her body, as she returned his kiss with innocent passion.

Dan's arms, hard, heavy bands of steel, slid around her, holding her tightly, his heart beating as fast as her own, pounding against her breasts.

PATRICIA LAKE
is also the author of these

Harlequin Presents

465—UNTAMED WITCH
501—PERFECT PASSION
521—WIPE AWAY THE TEARS
538—HEARTLESS LOVE

Many of these books are available at your local bookseller.

For a free catalog listing all titles currently available,
send your name and address to:

HARLEQUIN READER SERVICE
1440 South Priest Drive, Tempe, AZ 85281
Canadian address: Stratford, Ontario N5A 6W2

PATRICIA LAKE

LAKE

---

a step backwards

Harlequin Books

TORONTO • NEW YORK • LOS ANGELES • LONDON
AMSTERDAM • PARIS • SYDNEY • HAMBURG
STOCKHOLM • ATHENS • TOKYO • MILAN

Harlequin Presents first edition February 1983
ISBN 0-373-10570-3

Original hardcover edition published in 1982
by Mills & Boon Limited

CHAPTER ONE

THE sound of the doorbell broke Cathy's concentration, making her jump and ruining the careful line of colour that she was painting around her lips. She cursed softly, removing the smudged lipcolour with a tissue before getting to her feet to answer the door.

It was not like Greg to be early, she thought, wondering at her faint irritation and glancing at her watch as she ran nimbly downstairs to open the front door. It was not Greg who stood outside, however, but Joe, her brother. His long hair was plastered to his head, dark with rain, and he was leaning heavily against the door jamb. Cathy looked at him in silence for a moment, surprised to see him. There was something wrong, she could feel it in her bones. Joe was staring back at her with dull eyes, his mouth slack, clumsily forming words that she could not understand, and she realised in that second that he was drunk.

'Joe, what's the matter? What's happened?' There was a spark of urgency in her usually calm voice.

'Can I come in?' His words were very slightly slurred, he was making a big effort to sound normal.

Cathy pulled at his arm, unbalancing him, glancing out at the steady downpour that had started an hour ago and showed no signs of letting up.

'Yes, of course you can come in. You're soaked!'

5

Her voice was mingled with exasperation and concern, as the material of his brown corduroy jacket squelched beneath her fingers. Joe shook off her helping hand and came inside, almost making her smile at the intent concentration on his face as he walked past her with enforced, careful dignity.

She ushered him into the sitting room, still feeling her worry nagging away inside. Joe was not used to drink; she had never seen him in this state before, there had to be something dreadfully wrong.

She helped him out of his soaking jacket and made him sit down by the blazing fire.

'Quite a storm out there,' he smiled crookedly.

'I'll make you some hot black coffee,' she said briskly, containing her apprehensive curiosity because she knew from long and difficult experience that she would get nothing from her brother until he was ready to tell her.

In the kitchen she lit a cigarette as she waited for the percolator, drawing on it deeply, not noticing that she was tapping her foot with nervous impatience.

It could be that he had simply had too much to drink. It was quite ridiculous to worry so much about him. He was, after all, two years older than her, well old enough to look after himself, to sort out his own problems, but ever since their parents had been killed in a hotel fire three years ago, she had somehow felt responsible for Joe, protective, almost maternal.

She was fully aware that the helpless, beaten look he wore whenever he came to her for help was deliberately put on, but she always fell for it—every single time, without fail.

Tonight was different. He had been drinking and

even though she knew him well enough to suspect a ploy, a play for sympathy, she could not believe that he would go to such lengths to elicit her help.

The death of their parents had affected them both very deeply, bringing them together as never before. Cathy had known, young as she was, that Joe had suffered much more than she had at such a loss. He had become withdrawn, careless of his own safety, totally changed in personality. They had clung together, for the memories they both shared, for the memories they could give each other, and that was when Joe had come to rely on her.

Cathy could not blame him for the weakness she saw in him, it was an inherent part of his character. She loved him and wanted to help him, but it had been pointed out to her by several close friends that Joe had to learn to stand on his own two feet. He was twenty-two years old, a fully-grown adult man, he should be able to cope with his life, with his problems without running to a sister younger than himself, every time something went wrong. These well-meaning words rang in her ears now, as she stubbed out her cigarette and reached into the cupboard for two mugs. Her friends spoke the truth, and she realised that it did Joe no good to know that whenever he asked, she would always help him. But how could she refuse? He was her only family and most of the time she was only too glad to help him when she could.

She sighed heavily and loaded the percolator, mugs and cream on to a tray. It was an impossible situation.

Joe was slumped in the chair where she had left him, gazing moodily into the flames of the fire, when she re-entered the sitting room. He did not look up as she set down the tray and sat down opposite to him. She poured him some coffee, suddenly remembering Greg and their dinner date. Glancing at the clock, she saw that he would be arriving to pick her up in less than half an hour. She looked at her brother uncertainly. She could not leave him alone, not in his present state, and even if she went out with Greg, she would only be worrying about Joe, spoiling the evening for both of them. If she telephoned Greg's flat now, she might just catch him before he left.

She thrust the mug of coffee into Joe's cold hands and left the room to telephone. Luckily Greg was still there.

'Greg? It's Cathy. I'm terribly sorry, but I'll have to cancel tonight . . .' she began regretfully.

'Why?' Greg cut in, sounding impatient and rather annoyed.

'It's Joe. He's arrived here unexpectedly, he's drunk and very depressed and I can't leave him,' she explained, miserable at having to let Greg down. He was a good friend, he would have already booked a table at the restaurant, worked hard to make the evening enjoyable for her, and she felt cold and guilty ruining his plans. 'I'm sorry, Greg, I know it's short notice, I didn't mean to spoil your evening.' Her voice trailed off uncomfortably. There was nothing more she could say.

'It's all right, Cathy, don't worry. I do understand,' he said, disguising his disappointment in an effort to comfort her. 'Do you need any help?'

'No, I can manage.'

'I'll phone you at the weekend and perhaps we can arrange something for next week, what do you think?'

He rang off soon afterwards, and still feeling

rather guilty, Cathy went back into the sitting room to talk to Joe.

The coffee seemed to have done him some good, he seemed more relaxed and even managed a smile, as she poured out some coffee for herself and gracefully curled her feet beneath her in the low comfortable chair.

She looked at him, wondering what to say, how to begin.

He looked tired, she thought worriedly, her brown eyes idly following his careless movements as he lit a cigarette, offering her one which she refused. He was tall with a lean, strong physique and a thin animated face framed by long untidy brown hair, and Cathy felt a fierce rush of affection for him as she watched him smoke, watched the misery in his eyes.

'Any more coffee?' he asked, his voice purposefully light, avoiding her eyes as he held out his cup. She poured some out and he drank it in two long gulps. 'That's better. I'm beginning to feel quite human again,' he smiled ruefully.

'Joe . . .' she began, wondering how to broach the subject, but he did not let her finish.

'I'm sorry for just barging in without any notice, Cath—is it inconvenient?' His voice and face were worried, but he already knew what her answer would be.

'No, it's not particularly inconvenient,' she replied, smiling at him. 'What's the problem, Joe?'

He frowned. 'Were you going out?' He did not answer her question.

'I was, but now I'm not,' she explained patiently.

'Greg?' He seemed anxious to avoid the subject of himself.

'Yes, if you must know. You've been drinking—why?' she questioned directly, impatiently.

'I've been drunk,' he replied flatly, still not meeting her eyes, his gaze veering off towards the fire.

Cathy flicked a long strand of black hair over her shoulder. 'But why?' she repeated.

Joe shrugged. 'Why not? It seemed like a good idea at the time.' His uncaring smile made her angry.

'It doesn't seem like a good idea to me, at any time,' she retorted coldly.

'I'm beginning to think you're right.' Joe smiled. 'I'm sure I'll feel like death tomorrow morning.'

'It will serve you right,' she snapped, tired of his fencing.

'Don't worry so much, Cath, I'm feeling much better for that coffee. I don't suppose I could cadge a sandwich? I missed dinner.'

She raised her eyes in despair. 'You're impossible,' she said wearily. 'Would bacon and eggs do?'

Joe smiled wickedly. 'Bacon and eggs would do just fine.'

He sat in the kitchen, oddly silent, and watched her as she cooked enough for both of them. It was a scratch meal as she had been expecting to eat out.

'So when are you going to tell me what's wrong?' she asked carefully, nibbling a piece of toast as she watched him eating quickly and with obvious relish. Joe was silent for a few seconds. 'And don't tell me that there's nothing wrong, because it's obvious, to me anyway,' she added, aware that he would prevaricate for as long as he could.

Joe finished his meal and pushed away his plate

with a satisfied sigh. 'Can you lend me some money?' he asked, suddenly direct, but still not looking at her.

Cathy sighed an inner sigh of pure relief. She had imagined all kinds of trouble that he might be in, and by comparison, money seemed a minor problem.

'Probably. How much?' she asked, tucking into her bacon and eggs with renewed appetite. Joe was silent again and she smiled at him. 'Come on, tell me the worst,' she encouraged, still eating hungrily.

Her brother took a deep breath. 'Twenty-three thousand pounds,' he muttered, very quietly.

Cathy's dark eyes widened incredulously, her fork stationary, half way between her plate and her mouth. *'How much?'* She was breathless with amazement.

'Twenty-three thousand pounds,' he repeated slowly, his fingers playing nervously with the lace tablecloth, his attention seemingly engrossed in a loose thread.

Cathy's fork clattered to the table. She felt shocked, confused and rather hysterical. He couldn't be serious! She heard her own laughter, high and amazed.

'Is this a joke . . .' she began, and Joe raised his eyebrows.

'It's not a joke,' he said in flat desperation. 'I wish to God it was.'

She could only stare at him with wide, shocked eyes, totally speechless as the realisation hit her that he was *not* joking, that he actually *did* owe somebody twenty-three thousand pounds. Joe lowered his head into his hands, a tired, defeated gesture, and somehow this tiny movement, irrelevant though it was, sparked off Cathy's irritation with him again.

It was not the first time he had come to her in despair, but this time she sensed that it was very, very serious. She felt a strong sense of injustice that he should arrive drunk on her doorstep, forcing her to cancel a pleasant evening engagement with a friend, dropping a bombshell that she knew would keep her awake for many sleepless nights to come. And to cap it all, he had not even volunteered any information as to how he found himself in debt for such an *enormous* sum of money.

She picked up her fork from the tablecloth, throwing it back on to her plate, where the sight of her half-eaten food made her feel physically sick. She lit a cigarette, noticing in her anger that her hands were trembling slightly. Her brother had not moved.

'For God's sake, Joe, tell me about it!' she said, her voice unintentionally cold and rather sharp as she drew deeply on her cigarette, resenting the tightening in her stomach and the icy coldness that lay like a heavy stone in her chest. And even as she asked, she wondered if she really wanted to know.

Joe shrugged. 'I'm not proud of it, you know.' His mouth was sullen, his tone belligerent.

'Tell me,' she repeated with a sigh. 'From the beginning.'

Flashing her a martyred look, he said, 'A couple of months ago when I was still seeing Laura—remember, I told you about her?'

Cathy nodded silently, her imagination running riot again as she remembered the girl in question. Joe had come round to see her one Sunday evening bursting with the news of his latest romance.

Laura was a top fashion model, he had told her

proudly, pulling a glossy magazine from his coat pocket and showing her a fashion feature, wildly expensive designer clothes, modelled by a tall, ravishing, auburn-haired beauty, who was Laura. Joe had been excited and elated that this beautiful, successful woman had agreed to have dinner with him.

Cathy had been happy for him, ignoring the faint, elusive worry that had been nagging away at her, as she listened to him talk. Her brother had been infatuated, totally and utterly infatuated with Laura, and when after a few weeks he had casually let slip that the affair was over, that Laura had dropped him without a reason and was seeing the editor of a well-known international magazine, Cathy had comforted him, aware that he was deeply hurt, suddenly aware that he had fallen in love with Laura and that their parting had been a cruel, savage blow to his feelings, his self-confidence and his pride.

Since that evening he had not mentioned her, not once, and Cathy had hoped and suspected that he was beginning to get over the broken affair. But as he now mentioned Laura's name again, her heart sank as she forced herself to listen to his story.

'I wanted to impress her, I suppose. I took her to a casino one night—I had a couple of hundred pounds and I could hardly believe my luck. I seemed to win every time I played. I left the casino that first night with over two thousand pounds in winnings. It was so easy, so very easy—I was charmed, lucky, I couldn't lose.'

'Oh God, Joe!' Cathy wailed. 'How could you be so stupid?' It was hardly a tactful choice of words, and she did not mean to be so harsh, regretting her impulsive interruption as soon as she saw his young mouth tightening sullenly.

'I don't need you to tell me how stupid I am,' he muttered coldly, very defensively.

'I'm sorry,' Cathy said quietly, knowing that she had to tread carefully. He was sensitive and very touchy. 'Carry on. What happened?'

He got to his feet in a sudden jerky movement and began pacing up and down the kitchen, easily betraying his agitation.

'Laura enjoyed going to the casino—I'm not blaming her for the mess I'm in, though—so we started going regularly. I won the first few times, not a fortune, but enough to convince me that Lady Luck was on my side. And then one night I suddenly began to lose. I lost all the money I'd won and more besides. The casino gave me credit and I felt sure that if I carried on for long enough my luck would change again. Some hope! By that time I was hooked and within a week I'd lost more than I could possibly pay back. It had gone too far and I had to carry on, it was the only way to get enough money to pay off the casino—or so I thought,' he finished bitterly.

Cathy shook her sleek dark head in amazement, hardly able to believe her ears. 'And now you owe them   twenty-three   thousand   pounds,'   she murmured, almost to herself.

'Yes, and they won't let me play either.'

'I should think not!' she retorted in exasperation. 'If you hadn't in the first place you wouldn't be in this unholy mess.' She paused. 'What I don't understand is why they allowed you so much credit.' Joe was a very junior photographer with a national newspaper. He did not earn enough to merit such credit.

She looked up at him, watching the dull red flush creeping up his face.

'The manager is a personal friend of Laura's, and ... and I was putting on a big act, flashing money around, talking big, you know how it is.' Cathy didn't, and her tight, angry face told him so.

'Also, the manager knew that I was related to Dan Foreman. I guess that made me very credit-worthy.' His voice had dropped to an embarrassed, self-deprecating mumble.

Cathy's small face froze at the mention of Dan's name, a cold detached part of her mind marvelling at the sharp, tearing pain that the mere mention of his name could inflict on her, even after all this time.

'Dan's involved in this?' she whispered, her dark eyes desperate on her brother's face.

'No, he isn't involved at all,' Joe replied flatly, his own eyes sharpening on her white face. 'I didn't hide the fact that I was related to him, that's all. They assumed that any debts I ran up would be covered.'

'You deliberately let them assume that Dan would pay your gambling debts?' Her voice was high, perilously high and rough with pain, as she stumbled over Dan's name.

Joe moved uncomfortably. 'I thought I couldn't lose,' he muttered lamely.

She had to know. 'Will they go to him for the money?' She felt a hot tide of colour racing up her face at that thought. She could not imagine any-thing more humiliating, more shameful.

'No, I've made it clear that Dan won't give them a penny.'

'I suppose that's something,' Cathy said numbly, reaching for another cigarette and lighting it with cold careless hands. She had not thought of Dan all day, but as she inhaled on her cigarette, his hard, dark face rose up before her, making her shiver with a mixture of desperate need and terrible hurt, a feeling she was depressingly used to. Damn Joe for mentioning him now of all times, in the middle of a crisis.

With the last ounces of her will-power she forced thoughts of Dan out of her mind and tried to concentrate on the problem in hand. She could hardly believe her brother's recklessness in running up such an enormous debt, it was crazy and totally irresponsible, and however much she racked her brains she could see no solution, no way to pay back such a huge amount of money.

'A gambling debt is a debt of honour,' she pondered aloud. 'You're not legally obliged to pay it, and they can't sue you for it. Perhaps you could offer to pay it off bit by bit.'

Joe laughed humourlessly, raising his eyebrows in amazement at her naïvety. 'It's not like a bank loan or a hire purchase agreement, you know—I'm in big trouble. As far as they're concerned, I've been a naughty boy.'

'But surely they realise that you don't have that sort of money,' said Cathy, ignoring the sarcasm in his voice.

'They don't give a damn,' he replied flatly.

'What will they do?'

'They've given me a date by which the money must be paid. If I don't pay, it will be very nasty for me—very nasty,' he underlined with resignation and fear.

Cathy's head jerked up, staring at him. 'You mean . . .?' She stammered, appalled at the visions rising up in her mind's eye.

'Yes, that's exactly what I mean. I need help, Cath, and I need it now.'

She bent her head in thought, not knowing how to help him.

'I don't think I can help you, Joe,' she said quietly, after a moment or two. 'I haven't got that much money, although I could lend you a couple of thousand. I couldn't even get a loan on an amount that big.' A thought struck her. 'You said Laura was a friend of the manager, couldn't she put in a word for you?'

Joe coloured hotly, revealing the depth of his feelings. 'No. I don't know where she is anyway.'

'You could find out.'

'No.' He was adamant, very uncomfortable.

'I can't think of anybody who can help,' she said resignedly, miserably.

'You could help me,' said Joe, coming to kneel in front of her in an unconsciously beseeching position.

'How?' she questioned, reaching out to touch his cheek, her brown eyes very gentle.

'You could ask Dan for the money.'

It took a second or two for that to sink in, but when it did, her face paled, her whole body stiffening in rejection.

'No!' She shook her head in fierce determination.

'Why not? I'd pay him back somehow, and twenty-three thousand pounds would be nothing to him.' Her brother's eyes and voice were pleading, begging her for help that she could not give.

'If you think he'd give you the money, why don't you contact him yourself?' she asked shakily, pressing a cold, trembling hand to her forehead, feeling sick at the very thought of going to Dan for money. She couldn't! It was totally beyond her capabilities.

'You know damned well that he wouldn't give the money to me, he's never been particularly fond of me, especially as I never turned up for your wedding,' Joe said wryly. 'I probably wouldn't even get near him. But you . . . he'd give the money to you, I'd stake my life on it. Please, Cathy, Dan's my only hope. Won't you try?'

She closed her eyes against his persuasion, blindly shaking her head in amazement at his unshakeable confidence in her ability to get money from Dan.

'I can't,' she whispered painfully. 'Don't ask me to, Joe, please.'

He sighed. 'Don't you see that I have to? You can help me, Cath, and if you don't. . . .' He lifted his hands in an expressive gesture of promised violence, violence that she now had no doubt would be perpetrated against him if he did not pay off the casino by the given date.

She felt as though she was being pulled apart by wild horses. Joe was in serious trouble, begging for her help, giving her only two choices—to turn him away and be responsible for whatever happened to him, or to go to Dan and beg him for a loan. Both courses of action seemed utterly unthinkable, and her heart was beating painfully fast as she stared into her brother's face. She loved Joe and knew with utter certainty at that second that she could not let him down. She was the only person who could help him, she would have to bury her pride and all her hurt and go to Dan for help.

'What do you want me to do, then? Fly over to Los Angeles and ask him for the money?' she asked tonelessly, making it sound, in her misery, as easy as strolling down to the supermarket for a bag of flour.

The triumph she glimpsed in Joe's eyes as she looked up at him hurt her very deeply.

'You don't have to go to Los Angeles—he's in London at the moment, he arrived three days ago,' her brother informed her with a smile.

Cathy glared at him. 'You had it all worked out, didn't you?' She could not hide her bitterness. Joe had known that she would not be able to refuse him. He had won even before he mentioned Dan, he knew her that well, could manipulate her that easily.

She felt a scalding rush of tears behind her eyelids, wishing that she was stronger, harder, able to let her brother go without worrying so dreadfully about him.

Joe flushed uneasily. 'I don't like to ask you to do this for me, I know how hard it will be. . . .'

'You've no idea at all,' she cut in tearfully, angry with him for his eager, triumphant acceptance of her agreement to ask Dan for the money. Joe would not tell her not to go, to forget it, even seeing her anguish. He would push her, pester her, bully her, until she had done for him something that every instinct, every conscious thought screamed against.

'Maybe not, and I am sorry, but I had to ask,' he replied, sounding to her over-sensitive ears totally unrepentant, even belligerent, as though *he* was the injured party in this thoroughly sordid business.

Pain and well-justified anger was welling up inside her and she wanted Joe to leave before she either broke down completely or screamed at him that he must *never* ask her to do anything for him again.

'You'd better go. I'll ring you when I've seen

Dan and tell you his answer,' she managed in an even voice.

'Yes. Right. Er . . . when will you see him?'

Cathy swallowed with difficulty, fighting her urge to shout at him, hit him, unable to bear his persistence.

'I'll ring him tomorrow,' she promised through almost clenched teeth, jerkily getting to her feet and walking out of the kitchen to the front door, holding it open in silence. She had nothing more to say to Joe.

Uncomfortably, he stood on the doorstep, obviously waiting for some word of encouragement, reassurance that she could not have given him to save her life.

They usually kissed, embraced affectionately on parting, but tonight Cathy just wanted him to go. She felt cold, frozen from head to toe, and she did not want to touch him, feeling in some illogical way that he had betrayed her.

Joe stood perfectly still for a few seconds, his head lowered, then he turned away.

'Well . . . goodnight, Cath . . . and thanks,' he mumbled awkwardly, then he was gone, walking quickly towards the road without looking back.

Cathy watched him go with dull eyes, finally finding the energy to shut the front door and go back inside, walking automatically into the sitting room to curl up on the floor in front of the fire, not noticing for at least five minutes that her face was soaked with tears.

Finally, long choking sobs racked her body and she gave herself up completely to her sadness, releasing the pent-up emotion that had been building up ever since Joe had arrived. It felt like ages since she'd had a good cry and she did not check her tears until they dried up, leaving her drained, empty and surprisingly calmer.

She lit a cigarette and threw another log on the fire, her eyes faraway as she thought about the evening's events. She was dreading having to see Dan again, always assuming that he agreed to see her. She had hoped, foolishly she realised now, that she would not have to see him again, not for at least a long while, not until the pain had eased a little and her wounded heart was not so raw and vulnerable.

Her thoughts turned to Joe. She had agreed to help him, not only because she loved him and felt responsible for him, but because in a strange way she felt to blame for the way he was.

When their parents had been killed, Cathy had been rocketed into instant maturity, while Joe, desperate with grief, had clung to his adolescence. They had lived in their parents' house together and Cathy, young as she was, had become both father and mother to her brother. With no control or discipline, the weaknesses in his character had been allowed to develop unchecked. They had turned him into a wild, reckless young man, so reckless that his very safety now seemed threatened. Laura's rejection of him had not helped either.

Over and over in her mind, Cathy tried to think of another solution to the problem, a solution that would avoid any contact with Dan. But there was no other solution and she finally had to admit defeat, getting to her feet, feeling empty and very weary.

She would take a long hot bath and go to bed, knowing for certain that she would not sleep for hours. After running the bath, she slipped off her pink cotton dress and underclothes and soaked in the hot scented water for as long as she could, carefully keeping her mind as blank as possible, forcing herself to relax.

She dried herself slowly, examining her body absently in the mirrored tiles of the bathroom. She was tall and slender with a curved, perfect figure, her skin pearly white and unblemished. As she gazed at her naked reflection, memories of Dan's strong hands, his warm sensual mouth on her body, crept unbidden into her mind, and she felt the tautening of her breasts and the fierce warm ache in the pit of her stomach, with self-anger and misery. She bit her lip savagely and pulled on a pale silk nightdress, pretending to herself that if she covered her body, her longing would go away.

It didn't, of course, but she had lived for so long without Dan's lovemaking that she was quite used to squashing her needs, her desire for a man who did not love her.

If you're not careful, she sternly told her reflection, you'll end up a bitter, frustrated old spinster.

She combed out her long dark hair, letting it fall loose in shining black waves down her back, then washed her face and brushed her teeth. She looked as awful as she felt, she decided, as she applied some moisturising cream, totally unaware of her own sweet beauty.

Her eyes were still a little swollen from crying, but even red rims could not disguise the loveliness of evenly-spaced, large brown eyes, that held calmness and gentleness and reflected the deep, perceptive and amusing character beneath.

She had a small straight nose and a vulnerable, perfectly-shaped mouth above a small pointed chin. She was beautiful, but tonight, as on many other nights, she could not see that beauty, merely the well-known, boringly familiar features of a woman who had been crying far too much.

She grimaced at herself and went to bed, only to spend a troubled, uneasy night, haunted by dreams of Dan and their brief time spent together, dreams that she did not want to remember when she woke before seven to find her face wet with tears again.

She made some coffee, sipping it quickly, then, dressing in jeans and a red woollen sweater, went for a walk along the beach. It was deserted, apart from the odd early morning runner, and she walked along the edge of the water undisturbed, letting the cold sea splash over her small bare feet, gazing out towards the horizon at the pale, colour-washed sky of late dawn.

She enjoyed living on the coast, glad that she had bought the small stone cottage just a few miles outside Brighton, where she and Joe had been brought up. It had been like coming home, when she and Dan had parted. Joe lived in a flat in the town and she had many friends in the area. She walked briskly, breathing deeply the salted morning air, her ears filled with the screaming of the gulls overhead, and by the time she got back to the house it was after nine, time to ring Dan's office in London.

She found that she was shaking as she dialled the number, surprised to find that she easily remembered it. She did not want to speak to Dan himself, she still needed time to prepare herself mentally for that, so she asked for his secretary when the company answered.

There was a short silence, then a cool attractive voice said, 'Good morning, Mr Foreman's office. Can I help you?'

Cathy swallowed back the choking lump in her throat. 'Is . . . is that Mr Foreman's secretary?' she faltered, desperately trying to muster her self-confidence.

'Yes, Helen Gowers speaking.' Cathy did not know the name, the secretary must have been fairly new to the job.

'I'd like to make an appointment to see Mr Foreman this afternoon,' she requested briefly.

There was a slight pause from the other end of the line. 'Who is speaking, please?'

Cathy took a deep breath. 'Catherine Foreman,' she replied quietly.

There was another pause and she could almost feel the secretary's puzzlement.

'Would you like to speak to Mr Foreman?' There was something about Helen Gowers' cool voice that grated on Cathy's nerves.

'No . . . no, I'd just like an appointment for this afternoon, please,' she repeated patiently, her heart pounding out the question.

'Hold the line, please.' There was a faint click, then silence, and Cathy, gripping the receiver with white knuckles, felt the desperate urge to slam down the phone. She did *not* want to speak to Dan, she certainly did *not* want the appointment that she was requesting.

'Damn you, Joe!' she muttered to herself.

Helen Gowers came back on the line seconds later. 'Mr Foreman will see you at two-thirty this afternoon if that is convenient,' she informed Cathy politely.

'That will be fine. Thank you, goodbye.' She hung up quickly, knowing that she had not mistaken the interest, and perhaps a certain malicious amusement, in the secretary's voice. Miss Gowers had no doubt heard the gossip about Dan and Cathy; it would make the forthcoming interview even more difficult to face.

She showered and dressed carefully for her meeting with Dan, the first in eighteen months. She was glad that she had decided to approach him at his London office, it seemed to put the whole thing on a distinctly businesslike basis, which was what she would need if she was going to come out of all this in one piece.

She made up her face very carefully and looped her long shining hair into a neat chignon, before dressing in a pale green tweed suit with a cream silk blouse. The suit was cut in a simple, dramatic style, emphasising the smooth curves of her figure. She knew she looked good in it, which gave her much-needed confidence, its classic lines making her feel cool and poised.

She pinned an intricately-designed gold brooch to the lapel of her jacket and stepped into high-heeled shoes, then examined herself closely in the full-length mirror in her bedroom, schooling her features into calmness.

The effect was perfect, exactly what she had been aiming for, totally disguising her raw emotions, her uncertainty, her fear. The woman who stared back at her from the glass through clear brown eyes was chic and coolly sophisticated, obviously ready to handle any situation. If she had to see Dan again, at least he would never know what their meeting cost her. She turned away from the mirror and left the bedroom.

She had not eaten all day and she thought momentarily of food. It was probably not wise to travel to London on an empty stomach. The thought of eating made her feel sick, though, so she went straight through to her study to collect some papers and designs that she would be taking with her.

Since returning to England she had taken up her career again, and as an interior designer with a great deal of flair and talent, to say nothing of a few influential contacts, she was gradually building up her clientele and her reputation.

It was hard but satisfying and enjoyable work, the sort of career that she could throw all her energy into, exactly what she needed.

As she had to travel to London to see Dan, she might as well take the opportunity to drop in some designs to a client there, for approval.

She collected everything she would need and stored the papers and colour charts into a smart leather attaché case, after telephoning her client. Glancing at her watch as she lit a cigarette, she saw that she would have to leave for the station within five minutes. She had decided to take the train because she hated driving in the London traffic and parking there was practically impossible. She wanted a relaxing journey, arriving in London with her nerves and her temper in one piece. That was the theory, anyway!

Twenty minutes later she was on the train as it pulled out of the station. It was fairly packed with business commuters, but she had managed to get a window seat.

A handsome young man with a briefcase and a dark suit, sitting opposite her, was watching her with open admiration. Cathy flashed him a cold look and pulled out a newspaper from her attaché case.

In less than three hours she would meet Dan again. It was such a daunting prospect that she could not concentrate on the newspaper in front of her.

Her troubled gaze strayed out of the window. It was a bright, sunny day, the countryside green, peaceful and very beautiful.

Dan. He pulled her thoughts like pins to a magnet, and despite herself she found her mind straying back over their stormy, painful relationship.

CHAPTER TWO

At eighteen Cathy was at art college. She had managed to get a place at a Brighton college, when she left school, which suited her fine because it meant that she could continue living in her parents' house with Joe.

When she started there in the autumn term, she was full of hopes and dreams for the future. She enjoyed the social life and the carefree yet hard-working atmosphere of the college. It had been a little over a year since the death of her parents and she was just emerging from the long, dark tunnel of her grief into the sunlight again.

Everything seemed to be going well in her life, except for the occasional worry about her brother, who still suffered long periods of depression. Financially, they were very comfortable, having been left quite a large sum of money by their parents. Cathy also had her student grant and Joe had got a job on a small local newspaper.

During her second term at college Cathy applied for a six-month specialised course at a London college. Her application was accepted and although she was very apprehensive about leaving Joe alone, he urged her to go, reassuring and encouraging her. It was a big opportunity for her, as the course in London laid heavy emphasis on interior design, which was her choice of career, and luckily accommodation was no problem either because a close friend from her schooldays, Holly Bevan, now lived and worked in London and had offered Cathy a roof over her head for as long as she liked.

So Cathy moved into Holly's huge untidy flat, soon getting used to the bright hectic pace of the capital. She had only been in London for two months when she met Dan Foreman.

Holly arrived back from work one evening with a big smile on her face. Cathy was sitting by the window in the lounge, sketching the trees in the park opposite, and glanced up at her pretty friend.

'You look happy,' she remarked lightly, putting down her sketching book. 'Coffee?'

Holly nodded and sat down. 'Daddy phoned me at work today. He's throwing a party at the house on Saturday, and we're invited,' she reported enthusiastically.

Cathy handed her a cup. 'Me too?'

'Of course you too! It will be *fantastic*!'

'I can hardly wait,' Cathy smiled at her friend's excitement.

Holly's parents were divorced, and her father, a wealthy, influential businessman, had recently married a young, very beautiful actress. According to Holly her new stepmother threw '*the* most amazing' parties in London, hence her bubbling excitement. Cathy sipped her coffee calmly as she wondered whether or not to go. She did not have anything else planned.

Although many of the young men on her course had asked her out she had refused almost all of them. Some of them were attractive enough, but none of them really turned her head and she felt far too committed to her work at the moment to complicate her life with romance. She was cool, mature and level-headed, not wanting to become involved in sexual or emotional relationships—unless, of course, she met a man she knew she could love. And of the men who had asked her out, none of them fitted the bill.

Holly often teased her about her attitudes towards men. Beautiful, golden-haired Holly always had a man to go out with. 'I want to enjoy life to the full,' she told Cathy, 'and you should too. There's nothing serious going with half the men I see—it's just fun.' But Cathy shook her head. She enjoyed going out with a crowd of friends and sometimes a casual meal with a man, but she shied away from any further commitment with the men she saw.

It boiled down to the fact that she did not find any of them attractive enough, and she told Holly this. Her friend merely laughed, obviously not understanding. 'You're too serious,' she accused with affection.

She had been daydreaming and the sound of Holly's voice brought her head jerking upwards. 'I'm sorry, I wasn't listening,' she admitted ruefully.

'Are you coming with me on Saturday—to the party?' Holly repeated, raising her eyebrows in despair at the blank look on Cathy's face.

'Yes.' She made a quick decision. It would be nice to go to a party.

'Oh, good! I think I'll buy a new dress, I'm so *bored* with the ones I have.'

They talked until dinner, Holly relating amusing anecdotes from work that day, Cathy chatting about college. Holly worked for a television company as secretary to a programme researcher. She came into contact with many famous people and had a vast repertoire of scandalous and funny stories about them. She was a bright, vivacious, carefree girl, her personality a complete contrast to Cathy's quiet calmness, and they got on very well, a deep, strong and affectionate friendship lying between them.

Saturday came quickly, ending a busy week, and Cathy and Holly spent hours getting ready for the party.

Holly had bought a pink chiffon dress in a daring, backless style with a long floating skirt and Cathy had decided on one of her favourite party dresses, handprinted silk in muted shades of brown and grey, exquisitely patterned with a tight bodice, flaring skirt and thin velvet shoulder straps, also in grey and brown. It had been specially made for her by a friend on a fashion course at her college, reflecting the soft brown of her eyes and accentuating the rich lustre of her raven hair, while leaving bare her delicate white shoulders and arms. Unknown to her it gave her a graceful allure that drew male eyes whenever she wore it. She looped up her glinting hair, knotting it on the back of her head, leaving soft tendrils to caress her small jaw and vulnerable nape. Small grey ceramic earrings and grey high-heeled sandals completed her outfit and she did not wear much make-up, just a little pale eye-shadow and mascara and a colourless lip gloss.

She found that she was ready a full thirty

minutes before Holly and by the time they arrived at the impressive Victorian house, the party was in full swing, light and noise issuing from the stately building.

Cathy smiled and shook hands with Holly's father and beautiful stepmother Julia, then was suddenly swallowed up in the noisy crowd. She lost Holly in the crush, moving into a comparatively quiet corner of the room, clutching her glass and feeling rather shy, not seeing anybody she even vaguely recognised.

She was claimed almost immediately by a smiling blond-haired young man who seemed unable to take his eyes off her. They chatted as they moved to the loud, pulsating music and at the end of the dance, when the young man would have stayed at her side, Cathy politely excused herself and went in search of Holly, whom she finally found surrounded by a small knot of admirers.

Time passed quickly and enjoyably in the warm, smoky room. The food was delicious and Cathy found herself smiling a lot—she was happy.

She was talking to a friend of Holly's, a young man who had been round to the flat a number of times and whom she knew vaguely, when she suddenly found her eyes drawn to a tall man standing directly opposite to her, across the room. She tried to pull her eyes away before he noticed that she was staring at him, but found that she couldn't.

He was talking to a tall, redhaired woman, smiling at her, with a warm devastating charm that, even though it was not directed at her, took Cathy's breath away.

He was tall, well over six foot, with a powerful, virile physique that could not be hidden beneath the denim jeans and dark open-necked shirt that he wore.

Still talking to Holly's friend, Cathy watched the man throw back his drink in one careless mouthful, her eyes riveted to the contracting muscles in his brown throat. She let her wide, curious eyes wander over his face, drawn to this stranger almost against her will. Dark vital hair framed a lean, well-defined face. Hooded eyelids beneath thick dark brows, veiled grey-green eyes that were wise, amused and faintly world-weary. His mouth was firm and well shaped and Cathy took in every tiny detail of his face from the web of fine lines beneath his eyes to the flash of strong white teeth when he smiled.

He exuded an air of polished self-assurance, sophistication and wealth, and for the first time in her life Cathy felt an attraction so strong, so powerful, that it left her breathless, staring, rooted to the spot, until the man, as though sensing her wide, intent gaze, turned his head slightly and their eyes met, locking with an explosion of awareness that shot through Cathy's body like fire, tingling in every nerve ending, making her heart beat so fast that she thought she might suffocate.

The noise and the light in the room seemed to fade, the people blurring into a soft, brightly coloured mist, until she could see only the tall stranger, and it seemed that she could see him more clearly and with more piercing clarity than she had ever seen anybody before.

She was breathing in short shallow gasps as their eyes still held, a sweet, strange excitement rising deep in her stomach, and the tension, the shaft of fierce awareness between them seemed almost tangible, snaking across the smoky room, a solid entity.

Afterwards, Cathy could never say how long it lasted; it could have been only a second or two, it could have been years and years. Finally, as the noise and the light and the people began moving into focus again, intruding on them, the spell was somehow broken and with a supreme effort of will, she dragged her gaze away from those shadowed, unfathomable eyes, hot embarrassed colour washing up her small face, as she jerkily turned away.

She felt a bubble of hysteria rising up inside her. It was like the old song, she thought wildly, eyes meeting across a crowded room. Crazy.

Holly's friend was staring at her with puzzled exasperation, aware that she had not heard a word he'd said. She apologised, flashing him a brilliant smile, talking brightly and automatically, her mind still in turmoil.

She noted absently that the music had changed, it was slow and sensual now, the lights had been dimmed, throwing the room into smoky softness. She did not dare to turn round, but a sensitive prickling of the hairs on the back of her neck told her that the tall, dark man was slowly and inevitably moving towards her through the crowd.

Her whole body stiffened as she felt his hand on her bare shoulder, turning her to face him, his sure, gentle touch, liquid fire that seared right down to her toes.

She stared up into his shadowed, mysterious face, her brown eyes wide, innocent and a little frightened. Neither smiled, although Cathy longed to be able to.

The man's searching, smoky eyes moved over her small, uptilted face with an intimacy that held her spellbound, as though he too wanted to commit every tiny detail to memory.

'Dance with me,' he ordered softly, his voice low and sensual, American in accent.

Cathy did not answer but moved silently and gracefully into his arms, inextricably caught in a web of feelings and unknown emotions that she could not control or escape from.

They moved on to the dance floor, their bodies coming together sweetly and perfectly, moving as one to the slow, dreamy music. Cathy let her head rest lightly against his wide shoulder, the warm male scent of his body filling her nostrils, intoxicating her. Her heart was still beating very fast and she felt sure he would hear it as he held her so closely, his lean brown hands resting lightly but possessively at her waist and bare shoulder.

She could feel the powerful, leashed strength of his body against her own, the tensing of heavy muscles beneath smooth, thin cloth as she lightly touched his shoulders.

It was a dream, a warm hazy dream, she had never experienced anything like it before, and she relaxed against him, not mistaking the faint hiss of his indrawn breath and the tightening of his arms.

She lifted her head then, staring up into his dark face, smiling at him. He smiled back and she felt her pulses racing at the charm in that smile. He touched her hair gently. 'I don't even know your name,' he murmured.

Cathy laughed softly, knowing how he felt. Names did not matter at that moment, nothing mattered except their closeness, the sparking tension that crackled between them at the slightest contact.

'Cathy—Catherine Fairfax,' she replied in a soft lilting voice.

'Catherine.' He smiled as he quietly repeated her name. 'It suits you.'

'What's your name?' she asked, still staring up at him.

'Dan Foreman.'

She heard the transatlantic drawl again. 'You're American? I've never met an American before,' she admitted candidly.

Dan Foreman laughed. 'I've never met anybody as beautiful as you before.' The words should have sounded corny, hackneyed, but the veiled eyes were intent, his voice sure, gentle, giving a devastating sincerity to the compliment.

Cathy blushed hotly, lowering her eyes not knowing what to say, and heard his low growl of laughter as he caught her closer.

When the music stopped momentarily he did not let her go, but waited until it began again, and Cathy was glad, so very glad that he wanted to dance with her. She was feeling lightheaded, fiercely content to be with him, trembling slightly as his hand slid in one smooth, sensual movement from her waist to the warm bare flesh of her shoulder, his fingers caressing the soft skin of her nape.

Glancing up over his shoulder, her eyes suddenly met a pair of sullen, contemptuous blue ones, belonging to the tall redhead Cathy had first seen chatting to Dan. The woman was angry, her eyes avid on every small, indolent movement Dan made, and Cathy felt rather sick at such undisguised hunger, flinching at the malicious fury that shone in the blue eyes whenever they rested on her. It somehow spoiled her dream, for all she knew the redhaired beauty could well be Dan Foreman's wife, but she did not ask because, suddenly, she did not want to know.

Instead, when the music ended, she excused herself politely, murmuring an excuse about powdering her nose and left Dan's arms, shocked by the feeling of coldness, of sad loneliness, of losing something special and important, as he reluctantly let her go.

In the ladies' room she found Holly making repairs to her make-up. Her friend smiled at her, raising her perfect eyebrows in a curious, speculative movement. 'You haven't wasted any time,' she teased.

Cathy flushed, not meeting her friend's eye, examining her face closely and flicking an imaginary speck of dirt from her cheekbone.

'What do you mean?'

'Oh, come on—you've only been dancing with the most eligible man at the party for the last hour. Everyone's been talking about it,' Holly revealed delightedly.

'Dan Foreman?' Cathy could well believe that he was the most eligible man at the party, at any party, but she sensed that there was some other significance in Holly's words.

'Who else? Ninety per cent of the women here tonight would give their right arms to have spent the last hour where you spent it, and I don't mind admitting that I'm one of them.'

Cathy laughed, dispelling her slightly defensive feelings and relaxing. 'He is very attractive,' she admitted carefully, wondering whether or not to confide in her friend.

'And how!' Holly retorted emphatically.

'What do you know about him?' Cathy asked, throwing caution to the wind and giving herself up to the curiosity burning inside her.

Holly flashed her a superior, knowing smile. 'You mean you don't know who he is?' she squeaked.

'Obviously not. Who is he?' Cathy asked, calmly amused by her friend's amazement.

'Only you could dance so intimately with a man for over an hour and not know who he is!' Holly exploded in exasperation.

'So, tell me,' Cathy urged, pulling a comb out of her bag and tidying her hair.

'Dan Foreman,' Holly began in confidential tones, 'is a *very* famous oil millionaire—surely you've heard of him—everybody's heard of him!'

Cathy frowned, searching her memory as something sparked. 'Now you mention it, the name does ring a bell. Perhaps I've read about him in the paper—I don't know anything about him, though.'

Holly clucked her tongue reprovingly. 'Dan Foreman is front page news wherever he goes, Julia has probably pulled off the greatest social coup of the season, getting him here tonight—he doesn't attend many parties, so I hear.'

'But what do you know about him?' Cathy asked again, surprised by these revelations. The door opened as she spoke and a tall, thin brown-haired girl walked past them, glancing studiedly and obviously at Cathy before disappearing round the corner.

'See what I mean?' Holly smiled. 'I told you everybody was talking.'

Cathy grimaced. 'I don't want to know. Tell me about Dan Foreman,' she urged, wanting to steer the conversation away from the gossip about herself.

'Well . . . he's thirty-six, very, very rich, unmarried, so attractive that most women fall over themselves just to get a look at him in the flesh. He's been seen about with the most famous and beautiful women in the world. According to the papers, he can have any woman he wants, and frequently does,' Holly revealed with undisguised relish.

'A playboy.' Cathy wrinkled her nose with faint distaste, somehow unable to match up the man in whose arms she had danced with Holly's description. She was surprised at the relief she recognised in herself, on hearing that he was unmarried.

'I don't think so,' Holly said thoughtfully. 'He's worked hard, damned hard to build up his empire and he owns a number of companies over here, that's why he's in England at the moment. Even you must have heard of Foreman Incorporated.'

'Of course,' Cathy nodded absently. Foreman Incorporated was practically a household name.

'And women chase him, not the other way round—not usually, anyway,' Holly said slyly, her eyes curious again.

Cathy remembered the way she had stared at him, her face colouring with embarrassment again. Dan Foreman had probably thought she was just another predatory woman, after his blood, after his money. It was not a pleasant thought and one that she instinctively recoiled from.

'Do you know who that redhead is, the one he was talking to earlier? She's wearing a silver jump suit,' Cathy enlarged when her friend looked blank.

'Oh yes, that's Natalie Benjamin.'

'Girl-friend?' It was a shock to find what that question cost her to ask. It seemed dreadfully important that the unknown redhaired lady was not his girl-friend or his lover.

Fortunately Holly shook her head. 'No, not

from what I hear. According to Julia, she's some relation, cousin I think. She's part of the Foreman empire, works with the man himself.'

'Oh.' Cathy carefully digested the information, which did not really tell her anything, remembering the undisguised hunger she had glimpsed in Natalie Benjamin's eyes whenever she looked at Dan Foreman. Even if Natalie Benjamin was not his girl-friend, it was very clear that she had definite ideas in that direction and that she considered him her exclusive property. Cathy smiled to herself. It was impossible to imagine Dan Foreman being anybody's exclusive property.

He had affected her deeply, and as she realised how obsessively she had been thinking of him, danger bells began sounding in her head. She had never known herself to have such a strong interest in a man she did not know, and she felt instinctively that if she became involved with Dan Foreman she would be hurt. He lived in a different world from the one she inhabited, the huge gap between them would be difficult, if not impossible to breach.

It was time to retreat before he became too important to her. She'd had enough of the party, she would take a taxi back to Holly's flat.

She smiled at her friend. 'Sorry about all the questions. How about you, are you enjoying yourself?'

'I'm doing very nicely with second best, thank you, as you've sneaked in and grabbed first prize.'

Cathy laughed. 'Who's second best?'

'Garth, Julia's brother. Remember, I've had my eye on him since the wedding, I told you?' Holly's eyes were dreamy as Cathy nodded, remembering the man in question, tall and dark and very good-looking.

'He's asked me down to his parents' estate at the weekend,' Holly further reported.

'Really?' Cathy raised her eyebrows teasingly.

'To meet his parents, silly! They'll be there all weekend, worse luck,' Holly replied impishly. 'It's really rather strange, because not only are they his parents, but in a way they're my grandparents, or step-grandparents or whatever.'

'Interesting. You'll probably find that it's illegal for you to marry,' Cathy laughed, then yawned obviously. 'I feel worn out, I think I'll take a taxi back to the flat. You don't mind, do you?'

'You're not leaving!' Holly exclaimed in dismay.

'I am,' Cathy replied crisply.

'But what about Dan Foreman?'

'He'll have to find somebody else to dance with,' Cathy retorted uncaringly, knowing that the casual attitude was all a pretence. She did not even want to think of Dan Foreman dancing with another woman, especially if that other woman was Natalie Benjamin. Strange, dangerous feelings to have. It was definitely time to go.

'You're mad, stark staring mad!' her friend declared, then shrugged. 'Still, I suppose it gives the rest of us poor females a chance.'

'I wish you luck,' Cathy said flatly, picking up her handbag and turning to leave. 'I'll see you tomorrow.'

As she left the ladies' room to make her way to fetch her coat, Dan Foreman was suddenly in front of her, blocking her way, smiling down at her.

She stared up at him in surprise, her heart beating irregularly. He saw her surprise and laughed, running a gentle, careless finger down her cheek.

'I've been waiting for you,' he explained softly,

as though it was the most natural thing in the world.

Cathy swallowed nervously. 'You shouldn't have.' She managed a smile. 'I'm leaving now.' She cursed the pang of regret that accompanied those words.

'Let me drive you,' said Dan, still watching her intently.

'No, really, I can get a taxi,' she stammered, afraid of being alone with him, afraid of the fierce attraction that still held her in thrall.

She fixed her eyes on the top button of his shirt, fascinated by the fine dark hair that curled from the brown skin of his chest. Dan caught her small chin in strong fingers and tilted up her face.

'Catherine, I'll drive you,' he asserted in that soft drawl that turned her legs to water.

Looking up into the lean, dark beauty of his face, Cathy gave in. Why should she deny him? She wanted it as much, probably more than he did.

She smiled, unaware of her own beauty, the brilliance of her eyes, the faint, becoming colour in her cheeks, the vulnerable innocence of her mouth.

'Thank you,' she said quietly, watching the flare of light in his green eyes, with wonder.

She collected her coat and thanked Julia for the party, watching Dan as he made his goodbyes. Julia kissed his mouth lingeringly and it seemed that even Holly's beautiful stepmother was not immune to his attraction. Cathy turned away, not wanting to watch, her eyes absently scanning the room for a sign of Natalie Benjamin. She was nowhere to be seen. Cathy bit her lip. Miss Benjamin would not be pleased to hear that Cathy had left with Dan. The other woman would be a bitter enemy.

Moments later they left the house and Cathy

shivered as the cold night air hit her. It was freezing after the warmth of the house. Dan walked beside her with smooth animal grace, close, but not touching her. He did not have a jacket or a coat, but he seemed unaffected by the cold.

He opened the door of a low black car and she slid inside, huddling down into the seat, still shivering. Dan slid into the seat beside her, his hard thigh touching hers briefly, and switched on the engine and the car heater. She gave him her address as the car roared into life, speeding down the gravelled drive and on to the empty street. She felt shy, tongue-tied, as she fumbled in her bag for her cigarettes.

As if he could read her mind, Dan reached for a packet from the dashboard, offering her one, which she took, murmuring her thanks. The silence built up between them again as both smoked.

Cathy stared straight ahead out of the wind-screen, noting the effortless skill with which he handled the huge, powerful car.

'You're very quiet,' Dan said suddenly, his voice low, gentle.

'I'm sorry.' She stared at his strong, fleshless profile, sensing some criticism.

He flashed her a brief, devastating smile. 'Don't be—I like you the way you are.'

Cathy laughed and settled back into her seat again.

Ten minutes later the car slid to a silent halt outside the flat. Dan turned slightly in his seat, his arm resting lightly along the back of Cathy's seat.

'Thank you for the lift,' she whispered, desper-ately aware of him so near to her, aware of the intimacy of the car interior.

'My pleasure,' Dan drawled expressionlessly, the

green eyes careful on her face. 'Aren't you going to ask me in for coffee?'

'I . . . er . . . that is . . .' she stammered painfully, wanting more than anything to do just that, but unable to form the words of the invitation.

Dan watched her lowered head for a second, then caught her face, tilting it, his thumb moving caressingly against the side of her mouth, sensing her fear, knowing that he could not rush her.

She opened her mouth to speak, but his thumb moved softly over her lips, stopping her.

'Forget I asked,' he murmured, his eyes narrowing on her parted lips. 'Catherine.' He spoke her name very quietly, slowly lowering his dark head so that she felt his cool, clean breath against her hot skin.

His mouth brushed over hers gently, exploringly, once, twice, three times and she trembled violently, leaning towards him as he finally took full possession of her lips, his kiss deepening with a shock of desire that tensed his whole body.

Cathy moaned, a small stifled noise deep in her throat, as his mouth invaded with sensual expertise, her hands moving blindly to his powerful shoulders, clinging to him.

She had never received such a kiss before, and she was frightened of her own response to it. A shaft of awareness, of pure sexual excitement pierced her body, as she returned his kiss with innocent passion.

Dan's arms, hard, heavy bands of steel, slid round her, holding her tightly, his heart beating as fast as her own, striking against her breasts.

Then she was free, as he released her, closing his eyes and drawing in a long, faintly shaken breath. As she stared at him in confusion, his eyes snapped open and he smiled at her, his pupils still dark with what she now recognised as desire.

He lifted one of her hands, pressing warm, disturbing lips to the small palm.

'Have dinner with me tomorrow, Catherine,' he said softly.

'Yes.' She agreed immediately, following her instincts, wanting to see him again.

'I'll pick you up at seven-thirty.' He kissed her briefly, tenderly, then leaned over to open the car door for her, his arm accidentally brushing against the softness of her breasts.

Cathy smiled and slid gracefully out of the car, bidding him goodnight, her voice husky.

Later she lay in bed, staring into the darkness, her mouth still burning from his kiss, wondering whether or not she had made the right decision.

CHAPTER THREE

EARLY next morning when she woke Cathy felt full of energy, very restless, even though she had not slept particularly well. Holly was still asleep, not surprisingly, as Cathy had heard her creeping in well after four that morning.

She showered and dressed, than drank two cups of coffee, hardly able to sit down for more than five minutes at a time. Her feelings were alternating wildly from deep excitement at the prospect of spending the evening with Dan Foreman to fear, so nerve-racking that she wanted to telephone him immediately and cancel their dinner date.

It was impossible to settle down to any work, so

she decided to take a walk in the park. It was a crisp, blustery day, fluffy white clouds scudding across a clear blue sky. With her hair in a tidy ponytail and a thick woollen scarf around her neck, she walked for miles in an effort to burn off some of her nervous energy, feeding the ducks and geese on the lake and walking through the nearly-bare trees, her mind filled with thoughts and fancies about the man with whom she would be spending the evening.

When she finally looked at her watch she saw to her amazement that she had been walking for hours and that it was well into the afternoon. She walked back to the flat slowly, stopping on the way to buy some sweets, wondering what she would wear that evening.

Holly was watching television when she got back and putting the finishing touches to a dress she was making.

'Hello, how long have you been up?' Cathy asked teasingly, as she walked in, offering her friend a sweet from the bag in her hand.

'A little over an hour,' Holly admitted wryly, refusing a sweet with a shake of her golden head. 'Disgraceful, isn't it?'

Cathy laughed and pointed to the tray of coffee at Holly's feet. 'Any left in there? I'm parched!'

'Help yourself, then you can sit down and tell me exactly what's going on.'

Cathy had expected this, so shrugging off her jacket and scarf, she poured them both some coffee, then curled up on the floor in front of the fire, sighing with an air of mock-resignation that her friend did not miss.

'What do you want to know?'

'Everything,' Holly replied enthusiastically.

'I suppose we're talking about Dan Foreman.'

'Who else? When you said you were leaving last night, you didn't mention that you were leaving with the man himself. Which reminds me, those were delivered while you were out. The delivery man woke me up, otherwise I'd still be asleep now.' Holly pointed to a huge bunch of white roses, laid carefully on one of the chairs.

Cathy jumped to her feet with a small cry of delight, picking up the flowers, breathing in their beautiful scent and gently touching the velvet petals. There was a small card attached. She ripped open the envelope, already knowing that they were from Dan Foreman. Scrawled across the card in distinctive black handwriting he had written, 'Seven-thirty, Dan.'

She smiled secretly to herself, glancing round the room in search of her favourite vase in which to put the flowers. She arranged them carefully, aware of Holly's impatience, and placed them near the window, where the late afternoon sunlight fell on the unfurling blooms giving them a pure iridescent glow.

Then she returned to the fireside, her coffee and Holly's impatient 'Well?'

'I didn't know I was leaving with Dan. I intended leaving alone, but he offered me a lift, so I accepted,' she explained patiently. 'Any more questions?'

'The flowers?'

'They're from him.'

'When are you seeing him again?'

'Tonight for dinner, although I'm having second thoughts about it. I don't know whether I ought to go.' Her doubt shone in her eyes and Holly re-assured her.

'Oh, Cathy, don't you want to go? I'd jump at a chance like that.'

'Yes, I want to go, but I'm afraid of getting involved with him,' she admitted, glad that she had a friend to confide in.

'You're attracted to him—I've never seen a quarter of this interest in you before—and he's obviously attracted to you. You shouldn't worry so much, take things as they come. You'll only regret it if you cancel,' Holly said firmly.

Cathy thought about that, knowing that her friend was right, feeling reassured and almost certain that she was doing the right thing. 'Thanks. I needed someone to talk to.'

'Any time,' Holly said cheerfully.

'Did anything interesting happen after I left last night?'

'Not much, Garth and I were getting on *even* better by the end of the evening and—oh yes, Natalie Benjamin cornered me and asked who you were.'

'What?' Cathy was astounded.

'Oh, very subtly, of course, but it was obvious to anyone with eyes in their head that she was as mad as hell that Dan Foreman left with you.'

'Oh dear!' The last thing Cathy wanted was trouble; she was fully aware of the fact that she would never be a match for Natalie Benjamin.

'I shouldn't worry, there's not a thing she can do about it. I asked Julia about her too, and apparently she's been after Dan Foreman for years—with no success, it would seem.' Holly sighed enviously. 'You're *so* lucky.'

Cathy smiled. 'Maybe I am at that.'

'What's he like?' Holly was avid, relentlessly curious for details, but Cathy shrugged.

'Ask me tomorrow,' she replied, and Holly had

to give in. What could she say anyway? She hardly knew him at all. Physically, he was magnificent, he danced like a dream, he was gentle, charming and persuasive, hardly a detailed character analysis, and hardly enough on which to base the deep emotions she found he could induce in her. A strange fever ran in her blood and she had the feeling that events and circumstances were fast spinning out of her control.

She soaked in the bath for over an hour before she dressed for her date, still undecided on what to wear. After towelling herself dry and blow-drying her hair into a soft, shining cloud around her small face, she went through her wardrobe and finally chose a rich brown velvet suit with a fitted jacket and a full flaring skirt gathered into a wide waistband. It was chic and smart but special enough to wear for an evening out.

She made up her face carefully, then brushed her hair into a neat chignon, which she was well pleased with because it made her look older than her eighteen years. She dressed unhurriedly, teaming the velvet suit with an Edwardian lace blouse that she had bought in an antique shop in Brighton, and as a finishing touch added a gold brooch and gold earrings. She fastened her high-heeled brown shoes and was ready, nerves fluttering in her stomach as she looked at her watch and saw that it was only seven-fifteen.

Leaving her bedroom, she walked into the empty sitting room, Holly had already left for her evening date, and lit a cigarette, finding that she was pacing up and down as nervous as a kitten. She forced herself to relax, drawing on her cigarette, wondering whether or not a drink would help, but deciding against it. It would not do to greet Dan Foreman smelling of spirits.

The doorbell rang at seven-thirty precisely and Cathy visibly jumped, even though instinct had told her that he would be punctual. She stubbed out her cigarette with wildly trembling fingers and walked slowly to the front door, unprepared for the fierce rush of emotion that hit her as she opened the door and found herself in front of him.

He looked tall and powerful and devastatingly attractive in a dark suit, the informality of the previous evening gone. The suit was cut in a modern style, expensively tailored to his wide shoulders and broad chest, the slim-fitting trousers hugging his muscular legs.

Cathy stared at him for a moment, dry-mouthed, unable to speak, her heart pounding deep in her body.

Dan smiled at her. 'Hello, Catherine.' The low, drawling voice sent a shiver down her spine. Her wide startled eyes met shadowed green ones.

'H-hello. Won't you . . . won't you come in?'

He nodded, stepping into the narrow hallway, almost touching her. She backed away jerkily, moving ahead into Holly's flat, feeling totally inadequate and very stupid. If only she could talk normally to him, laugh with him, lighten the atmosphere somehow.

They reached the sitting room and Dan looked round with interest. Cathy managed a tight smile. 'Thank you for the roses, they're very beautiful.'

Dan stared at her, his eyes smoky, unsmiling. 'I'm glad you like them.'

'Would you like some coffee, a drink? We have some Scotch or some vodka. . . .' She broke off, biting her lower lip, listening to herself talking and realising that she was chattering on far too much.

'Scotch would be fine. Straight.' She was glad to have something to do, even though her hands shook alarmingly as she held the bottle to the glasses, deciding to have one herself.

Dan watched her every movement as he leaned indolently against the carved mantelpiece. As he took the glass from her their hands touched briefly and Cathy drew back as though scalded, the faint brush of his cool fingers tingling through her. He raised his glass to her in silent salute and swallowed back the whisky, his eyes travelling over her in slow appraisal.

'You look very beautiful,' he said softly, as his eyes returned to her small, flushed face. 'Th-thank you.' Cursing, she knew how inane she sounded, stammering her thanks for that breathtaking compliment.

Dan put down his glass and walked slowly over to her, his hands reaching out to rest lightly on her shoulders.

Cathy, acting without conscious thought, gazed up into his face with wide eyes.

'Don't be afraid of me, Cathy,' he murmured gently.

'I'm not . . . I can't help it,' she amended in a whisper, unable to lie to him.

He lowered his dark head slowly, brushing her mouth with cool lips. 'I'll never hurt you,' he murmured against her mouth, his warm breath fanning her cheek.

Much later, Cathy would remember those words, words that she had believed so utterly, so completely, with bitterness and misery, but then she smiled at him with shy, beautiful eyes and said, 'I know. It's just that I feel so shy, I don't know what to say to you. I wish. . . .'

Dan stopped her with his mouth, kissing her briefly, fiercely. 'Don't wish for anything. Come out with me now.' He took her hand in his, only giving her time to collect her handbag before leading her outside to his low black car, making her laugh, deliberately relaxing her, as they drove into the brightly lit city towards the restaurant of his choice, which, as Cathy had suspected, turned out to be an exclusive, expensive place that she had only read about before, never imagining that she would ever dine there.

The head waiter fluttered round them, fussing, falling over himself to accommodate Dan, who he obviously valued as a customer. The restaurant was boldly and exquisitely decorated and Cathy's artistic eyes slid round appreciating the colours, the small touches that gave the place such style.

Several other diners watched with interest as they were shown to their table, obviously recognising Dan, and Cathy almost smiled as she tried to imagine what they would make of her. A number of women were watching Dan openly, assessing his obvious and powerful potential as a man, as a lover. He drew female eyes so effortlessly that Cathy wanted to place her arm possessively in his, to show those hungry ladies that for tonight at least, Dan was hers. She stopped herself short, shocked by her own thoughts, blocking them from her mind as she sat down at their secluded intimate table.

Sipping drinks, they ordered their meal and, scanning the menu, Cathy realised that she hadn't eaten all day. She felt ravenous, and ordered melon followed by coq-au-vin. Dan ordered smoked trout and roast beef, telling her how he enjoyed English food. It reminded Cathy that he was American.

'Where do you live in America?' she asked curiously.

'My home is in Los Angeles, that's where I was born, but I spend a lot of my time in New York and Texas for business reasons,' he replied, offering her a cigarette.

Cathy accepted, her eyes on his lean brown hand as he held out a gold lighter to her. Everything he owned, down to the very smallest item, was expensive, the best money could buy. She looked at him, still curious, exhaling a stream of smoke through parted lips. 'You're very rich,' she said half to herself, blushing furiously as she realised that she had spoken aloud and that Dan was amused.

'How do you know?'

'I asked Holly about you,' she replied honestly.

'And what did she tell you?' Dan asked expressionlessly, his green eyes still gently amused.

'She told me that you were rich and famous,' Cathy replied, smiling at him candidly, making him laugh.

'Perhaps I should ask her about you, or will you tell me yourself?' he coaxed softly.

'I don't know what to tell you, there's nothing very interesting about me.' She felt more relaxed as she sipped her wine, feeling its warmth spiralling round her tense body.

'Everything about you interests me,' Dan said quietly. 'Tell me about your childhood. Do you have any brothers or sisters?'

'I have a brother, Joe, he's two years older than me, and he works for a newspaper. I'm only staying with Holly for six months, really I live in Brighton with Joe,' she explained with a smile.

'And your parents?' Dan probed, making his interest in her obvious.

'My parents have been dead for eighteen months,' she replied, still finding the words difficult to say, a frown pleating her smooth, pale forehead.

Dan sighed, taking one of her cold hands in his. 'I'm sorry.'

She flashed him an over-brilliant smile. 'I'm nearly over it now,' she said, not knowing that her bruised eyes were making a liar of her. 'I don't want you to be sorry for me.'

'I'll do my best,' said Dan with amused tenderness.

The waiter served their food at that moment and conversation stopped for a while as Cathy tucked into her ginger-sprinkled melon with relish.

'I'm starving,' she admitted, glancing up to find Dan watching her. 'I didn't eat all day because I was so nervous about seeing you tonight.'

'Nervous?' He picked up the word curiously.

Cathy grimaced, a faint flush stealing up over her face. 'I wish I wasn't so honest, words seem to pop out of my mouth before I notice. I'd never make a diplomat!'

'Would you want to?'

She laughed. 'No, but I'd like to cut down on the embarrassment my tongue causes.'

Throughout the meal, the wine flowed freely and Cathy drank more than she intended to. It seemed terribly important that Dan liked her, found her good company and without the inhibition-freeing wine, she found herself shy, tongue-tied and no doubt very boring to a man of his worldly experience. Under the influence of the wine, she became talkative, faintly flushed, her brilliance commanding all Dan's attention. It seemed as though he could not drag his eyes away from her, and under his gentle questioning, she unknowingly revealed all the details of her life, all her secrets to him.

He listened with rapt interest, his green eyes serious, intent and often shadowed with desire as they rested on her animated face and graceful hands. Cathy was beautiful and witty, with a shy, natural charm that ensnared him as they sat together, cocooned in their own interest in each other, both unaware of the people around them.

For dessert Cathy chose savarin with fresh cream and Dan ordered cheese and fresh fruit.

'I seem to have told you everything, so now it must be your turn,' she smiled at him.

Dan shrugged, lifting his broad shoulders eloquently. 'I was born in L.A., you know that already. Some of my family still live there—my father's a politician, my mother died ten years ago. I have two brothers, Tom and Kevin. Tom lives on Tahiti, I hardly ever see him, and Kevin lives in Canada and runs a printing company. That's my family in a nutshell,' he finished with a smile.

Cathy raised her eyebrows, fascinated, but wanting to know more. 'That doesn't tell me very much,' she reproved him gently. 'Tell me about you.'

'I was brought up with my brothers, we were all very close then, I remember it as sunny and wild and carefree. I went through college, to Harvard, was drafted into the army and sent to Vietnam, then I worked and hitchhiked my way round the world with Tom, that took four years, believe it or not, and when I got back to the States, I set up business and began making money, working hard. And here I am.' It was a very brief history of his life, but his voice, his eyes, his facial expression told Cathy a lot.

He was tough and self-sufficent with a powerful inner drive for wealth and success. His life, so different from her own, had moulded him into the sophisticated, intelligent and successful man who now sat opposite her. He had learned to harness the wild spirit inside himself without destroying it, as so many people did. He knew what he wanted and she guessed that he invariably got it. She imagined that he would be cold, calculatingly ruthless in pursuit of his desires, but she had glimpsed a warmth, a gentleness in him that was overpoweringly attractive, when coupled with the other qualities that formed the basis of his complex, forceful character.

She wanted to get to know him, it was the first time she had ever felt like that about a man. Dan Foreman attracted her physically and with his intelligence, his personality he was a potent combination, one that she was powerless to resist.

After coffee and liqueurs they both sat back, replete and relaxed, Dan smoking a cigar, the rough fragrance appealing to Cathy's nostrils, and she a cigarette. He smiled at her and unselfconsciously she returned that smile, still feeling a little lightheaded but very happy.

Their eyes locked as they had done at that first meeting, his shadowed, searching, hers wide, free of deceit. Both felt the dizzying tension building up, the sweet excitement that neither could control.

Cathy felt as though she was drowning in that deep green gaze that seemed to see right inside her, piercing her, breaking down all the barriers she had erected to face the world. She ached to touch him, for him to touch her, to kiss her, possess her. It was madness, because she hardly knew him, and her eyes dropped suddenly, breaking the electric contact, her gaze fixed on her hands, faint, tell-tale colour streaking her pointed face.

'Shall we go?' She heard his low cool voice with a shiver of awareness.

'Yes.' It was all she could manage, as she got to her feet. She looked at her watch and saw that it was nearly midnight. The time they had spent over the meal had flown past, lost for ever now.

Dan took her hand as they left the restaurant, pulling her close to him as they strolled towards his car, his thumb moving rhythmically against the sensitive skin of her wrist, disturbing her.

Once inside the car he turned to her, the strong dark planes of his face mysterious in the dim light.

'What would you like to do?' he asked with a slow smile.

'I ought to get back, I have to be up early for college tomorrow,' she answered regretfully.

'Right.' He seemed content to let her control the pace of events between them. He was aware of how easy it would be to frighten her off and he did not want to lose her.

He drove speedily and skilfully back to Holly's flat, and they did not talk much. Their silence was companionable; Cathy still felt relaxed and content and rather drowsy. Dan moved slightly, as they stopped at a red light so that she could rest her head against his shoulder. She nestled against him, fine strands of her shining blue-black hair clinging to the sleeve of his jacket, feeling his warmth, the deep, steady rise and fall of his chest as he breathed. She was almost asleep by the time they reached the flat.

The car slid to a silent halt and Dan gently shook her arm. 'Catherine, wake up, you're home!'

Her eyes flicked open in surprise, she stared into his strong face for a second, then moved her head quickly away from his shoulder, feeling embarrassed.

'Would you like some coffee?' she asked in a muffled voice, frightened that he would refuse. She did not want him to go, wanted to spend a little more time with him. She fervently wished that she had not suggested returning home so early.

'Yes, I would like some coffee,' Dan smiled.

The flat was in darkness as they walked inside, Holly was still out with her date. Cathy switched on the lights, glad to see that the fire was still burning. She moved to put some more coal on it, but Dan stopped her. 'I'll see to it,' he said, firmly but gently. She watched him for a second, then went into the kitchen to switch on the percolator and when it was ready, carried the loaded tray back into the sitting room, to find Dan standing by the window, staring outside looking curiously alone, but dominating the whole room with his presence. He drew her eyes.

'The . . . the coffee's ready,' she said falteringly, not really wanting to disturb him.

He turned immediately and the moment was gone, strolling smoothly across the room to sit next to her on the couch.

She noticed inconsequentially that he had loosened his tie, it now hung round his neck, and opened the top button of his shirt. She reached for the cups, knocking one over in her nervousness. 'Black or white?' she asked, her voice barely above a whisper, his nearness disturbed her so.

'Black, no sugar,' he replied, watching her trembling movements closely, finally reaching out and staying her shaking hand with his own.

'Catherine,' he groaned her name huskily, and brought her hand to his lips, kissing the palm, sending a wave of feeling through her. His other hand moved to her head, expertly pulling the pins from her neat chignon, so that her raven hair cascaded down about her slender shoulders, wild and free. He threaded his fingers through its heavy softness in a slow, sensual movement, finally tangling his hand in it to bring her head closer, until it was only inches away from his own. Cathy swayed towards him, unaware of her own actions, desperately needing the touch of his mouth, as he moved to kiss her.

He parted her lips with brief, hungry kisses, his mouth gentle, warm, sending fierce tremors through her body, then with a hoarse groan he took complete possession of her parted lips, his kiss deepening, hardening as he pulled her fully into his arms. Cathy responded completely, her mouth untaught yet passionate beneath his. She knew somehow, that since the last time he had kissed her, she had been waiting and waiting for him to kiss her again.

Of their own volition her arms crept around his strong neck, her slim fingers tangling in his thick, dark hair. He explored the inner softness of her mouth sweetly, his heart pounding against her body, then his mouth left hers, trailing urgently over her cheeks, closing her eyes, skimming over her forehead in slow caress, down to the sensitive lobes of her ears, murmuring her name over and over.

Cathy clung to him, her head arched back in surrender, desire for him roaring in her blood, knowing that he was fiercely aroused and losing herself in that knowledge. She pressed her lips to his throat, feeling the muscles there contracting as she did so.

Dan found her mouth again, his hands stroking down over her body, slowly, as though he was afraid of frightening her, his fingers traced every curve of her perfect figure, and she moaned softly as he possessively cupped her breasts. She could feel the tension in him, the rigid control he was keeping over his body, and she was lost in feeling, not responsible for her actions, as her own hands moved down to his wide shoulders, sliding beneath the expensive jacket of his suit to the thin silken material of his shirt, through which she could feel the smooth warmth of his skin.

She shaped the tense, powerful muscles with tentative fingers, wanting to give him pleasure, but suddenly his hands came up, closing over hers, trapping them into stillness against the unyielding wall of his chest.

'I want you, Cathy,' he muttered unevenly, all at once very still, as he fought to regulate his breathing. She smiled at him, her eyes sensual, tempting. 'I want you too,' she admitted huskily, satisfied with the responding flame that leapt in his green eyes as she spoke.

'You don't know what you're saying,' he said, his voice ragged, as with one lithe movement, he released her hands and got to his feet, walking away from her, searching in his pocket for some cigarettes.

She stared at him in confusion, too weak with sensual lethargy to move, her eyes wide, inviting, her mouth still swollen from his kiss.

'I think I do,' she said quietly, and realised in that split second that he had rejected her offer of love, moved away when she would have given him the only thing she had to give—herself.

Wild, hot tears filled her eyes, a product of her aroused and highly strung emotions. 'You . . . you said you wanted me,' she accused the long, tense sweep of his back. 'But it's not true, you don't want me at all. . . .' Her voice broke and she began to cry in earnest, not knowing what she was saying, she was too upset. Dan spun round on his heel, flinging his cigarette into the open fire in a violent movement as he moved beside her, swift with concern, taking her back into his arms, pressing her wet face to his shoulder as he comforted her. Although she tried, Cathy found that she could not control her tears, long sobs shook her body as all her pent-up emotion was released at last.

Dan pushed back her hair from her face, wiping away her tears with gentle fingers, murmuring low, soothing words that did comfort her, as she rested within the strong circle of his arms, fighting for control of herself. Finally she pulled away from him, quiet now, but feeling very embarrassed and extremely silly. What would Dan think of her hysterical behaviour? It did not bear thinking about. Holly's words rang in her ears. 'Women chase him, not the other way around.' It was especially true in her case, she thought self-deprecatingly. Not five minutes since she had offered herself to him on a plate, unconditionally, so great was his expertise, his careless power over her emotions.

She raked a trembling hand through her untidy hair, pushing it back from her damp, tear-stained face, only wishing that he would go and leave her to face her humiliation alone. He was making no move to go, though, he was beside her, silent, probably waiting for her to say something. She supposed it was better to get it over with, then he

would go, so she took a deep breath and said falteringly, 'I—I'm sorry, terribly sorry for what
happened. I don't usually act this way, in fact. . . .'
Her tongue was running away with her again and
she could not stop it.

'Cathy.' Dan cut across her, taking her shoulders
and turning her to face him, unwillingly forcing her
to meet his stormy green eyes. 'Don't apologise,
you have nothing to apologise for—it was all my
fault, I was clumsy, tactless, and if I hurt you, I
swear I didn't intend to. Think about it. If we'd
have made love just now, you would have hated
me afterwards. I don't want that.' His voice was
incredibly gentle, as gentle as the strong hands
resting on her shoulders. He was right, of course, it
seemed he knew her better than she knew herself.

'Dan, please. . . .' She wanted to tell him that he
had no reason to apologise either, the fault *had*
been hers, all hers.

He stopped her in her tracks before she had time
to finish the sentence, brushing her cheek with
warm, hard lips, easily disrupting her train of
thought.

'How can you think that I don't want you?' he
asked softly, wonderingly. 'You're beautiful, so
very beautiful, and God knows I do want you. Ever
since I saw you across the room at that party,
you've been haunting me. So don't tell me I don't
want you.' He smiled into her wide, surprised eyes.
'Or I may be tempted to prove to you just how I
do feel!' Cathy laughed, touching the hard bones
of his face with shy fingers. Suddenly everything
was fine again. He had been thinking of her, not of
himself, and everything was so good, so right that
she wanted to fling her arms round him. Of course
she didn't, she merely said quietly, 'I mis-

understood, I didn't realise—I'm sorry.'

Dan smiled again and briefly kissed her mouth. 'Let's forget it,' he suggested drily, and Cathy was all in favour of that, as he bent in a fierce hungry movement to claim her lips once more.

*

CHAPTER FOUR

DURING the month that followed, Cathy saw Dan almost every day. He seemed unable to leave her alone for more than twenty-four hours at a time, and that suited her very well, as she was utterly lost in her growing need for him.

She had no doubt that his work was suffering, and her attendance at college had become almost non-existent, but none of that mattered, the only important thing being that they saw as much as possible of each other.

Dan took her sailing, walking, visiting galleries and exhibitions, to theatres and restaurants, visiting friends, and seemed jealous of her time. He was openly courting her, sweeping her off her feet with his natural charm, his warmth.

Cathy's life became a dream, as she fell in love for the first time in her life. She found it difficult to believe the depth and strength of her emotion for him. No man had been able to raise a spark inside her before, and she had almost despaired of ever falling in love, the sort of love she had read about and secretly longed for.

Sometimes she felt frightened and unsure, wondering how long it would be before Dan tired of her. She was nothing special, she thought, and how

could she, an ordinary eighteen-year-old girl hope
to hold the affection and the attention of a powerful, successful man such as Dan? But her doubts
were always dispelled when she saw him, her pulses
racing as he smiled in greeting, as he drew her into
his arms and showed her a hunger and a need for
her that he did not bother to conceal. They had
not become lovers, even though Cathy would have
given herself to him in love and innocence, any
time he demanded it. Dan did not demand it, he
always drew back, using iron self-control to dis-
entangle himself from her soft white arms, when
she would have pulled him down to her again. That
he wanted her desperately was beyond doubt, and
there was a sweet triumph in the knowledge that
she could arouse him so, coupled with the warm
realisation that he respected her, hence his control.

Then, one fine Indian summer afternoon, the
situation between them changed. They had driven
to the country and lunched at an old riverside inn.
Revelling in the unexpected warmth and sunshine,
Cathy suggested a walk after the meal and smiling
indulgently, Dan agreed, taking her hand as they
cut across the fields. The sun was high, amazingly
bright and warm for the time of year, the sky clear
and blue. Cathy struggled out of her velvet jacket,
feeling hot and sticky, watching with caught breath
as Dan also removed his jacket, under which he
wore only a sleeveless black tee-shirt. She stared
dry-mouthed at his bare brown shoulders, his
smooth tanned skin gleaming in the stark light and
at the flexing of the powerful muscles in his arm as
he lazily hooked the discarded jacket over his
shoulder.

His body was magnificent, she thought hungrily,
as her glance skimmed over his hard stomach, the

strong length of his legs and lean hips encased in tight, faded jeans. She wanted him—oh, how she wanted him!

As her eyes returned to his face she saw that he was watching her, saw the all-consuming flame in his rare green eyes as he recognised her desire. She licked her lips nervously, unwittingly provocative, drawing and holding his fierce gaze on her tender mouth, as they both became trapped in a moment of explosive tension.

Finally Dan broke the spell, drawing a long heavy breath and taking her hand again as they began to walk on. It can't go on like this for much longer, Cathy thought desperately, as she tried to fight the weakness in her legs. It was like walking on a tightrope, one or both of them would surely fall.

They walked on for twenty minutes until they reached a shady copse, the grass dry and warm. Cathy pulled her hand free and sank on to her knees, not wanting to walk any further.

'I'm tired,' she said, sweetly plaintive. 'Can we rest?'

'Sure.' Dan crouched down gracefully, leaning back against a grassy bank. He rested his hands behind his head, staring lazily into the sky. Cathy leaned back too, closing her eyes, the sun bright behind her eyelids.

It was quiet and peaceful and hot, a day out of time. A late insect, brought out by the weather, buzzed slowly past her ear. It could have been midsummer, she thought contentedly, her mind becoming relaxed and drowsy. Absently she heard Dan moving and opening her eyes with reluctance she found him beside her, only inches away, propped up on one elbow, staring down at her with heavy, unsmiling eyes.

Her heart began to hammer wildly as he reached out and stroked her cheek, his fingers hard-skinned, gently abrasive, arousing.

'Dan, love me,' she whispered achingly, at the mercy of her own love for him.

She heard his soft groan as his mouth immediately found hers, parting her lips with urgency and expertise. He kissed her lingeringly, fully, his mouth warm, hungry and strangely fulfilling.

Cathy clung to him blindly, lost in sensation, her fingers exploring the smooth taut skin of his shoulders. Dan's mouth moved caressingly to her throat, his hands slowly unbuttoning her blouse, pushing it from her slender shoulders so that she was naked to the waist, the sunlight warm and dappled on her white skin, breathing unevenly as his glittering eyes rested on her bare, rounded breasts.

'Dear God, Cathy, you're beautiful! I have to have you, you're driving me insane,' he muttered harshly, torment in his voice, in his face.

She was mesmerised by his need for her, by her love for him, knowing with deep certainty that for as long as she lived, she would never, never be able to deny him.

She wanted to touch him, reaching out her hands to pull the tee-shirt from his powerful body, her heart stopping altogether for a split second as she looked at the hard lines of his tanned, hair-roughened chest.

Dan pulled her into his arms then, their bodies coming together perfectly, beautifully, holding her so closely that she could barely breathe, his hands moving slowly over her back.

She felt the convulsive shudder that ran through

him, and tightened her own arms around his waist, loving him so very much. His mouth sought hers again, blindly, fiercely as his hands explored her half naked body. She clung to him, the blood in her veins quickening, turning to molten fire, moaning softly as he touched her breasts, his hands gently stroking over her hardening nipples, trembling slightly against her heated skin.

He drew a long hoarse breath, suddenly taking her hand and pressing it to his chest.

'Touch me, Cathy, kiss me—give me your warmth, your love,' he whispered deeply, touching his mouth to the pulse that beat frantically in her throat. She sighed as she lightly ran her fingers through the rough dark hair that matted his chest, in a teasing, caressing movement, hearing him catch his breath raggedly. Her need to give him pleasure was a warm ache in her heart. His skin was warm and smooth and beautiful, and she gradually became bolder as she realised how she could affect him. His heart was racing beneath her stroking hands, beneath her mouth as she kissed his chest, tasting his skin, her head filled with the clean male scent of his body.

Dan's arms tightened involuntarily around her, muscles tensing, aware that within a few seconds they would both lose control.

The sound of a dog barking loudly, seemingly very near, broke between them. Cathy stiffened, fearing intrusion, coherent thoughts sliding slowly and painfully back into her mind.

'Dan. . . .' she began worriedly.

'Hush, Cathy, there's nobody coming this way,' he replied reassuringly, still holding her tightly. But he moved then, rolling over so that he lay beneath her, her head against his wide bare shoulder, his mouth moving against her hair.

Cathy swallowed, feeling very vulnerable and inexplicably close to tears. Somehow the moment had gone, the fear that someone would find them entwined in each other's arms, making love in this summer copse, had ruined her mood, making her nervous and as stiff as wood in Dan's warm, strong arms.

'Cathy.'

She looked up into his lean face, her eyes glowing with love for him. 'Mm?' she murmured drowsily.

'I want you to marry me, as soon as possible.' He stopped her as she opened her mouth to speak. 'I know I'm too old for you—God knows, I've been thinking about that ever since I met you, but I find I can't let you go. You're mine, you'll always be mine.' His hands moved possessively on her bare skin, reinforcing his harshly spoken words.

'Dan, my love, how can you think you're too old for me?' she asked softly, genuinely surprised, her heart burning with happiness as she flicked her tongue against his shoulder.

'I am,' he replied raggedly. 'I'm nearly twice your age—it's not a very good deal for you. You need a younger man, I know that, but the thought of you with anybody else. . . .' He paused, closing his eyes as though terribly weary. 'I just can't take it,' he admitted through clenched teeth.

Cathy touched his face tenderly, feeling the hard bones tightening beneath her fingers. She felt unable to bear his torment. Age meant nothing to her, it was strange that he laid so much importance on it. She loved him, she knew that now for certain, and that was all that mattered.

'Yes, I'll marry you—any time you want.' She smiled into his eyes, incredibly beautiful in her tenderness. Dan swallowed and kissed her mouth fiercely.

'Tomorrow?' he demanded huskily.

'Yes, tomorrow,' she agreed, kissing him back.

'Cathy. . . .' He murmured her name against her lips, his heavy body tautening against hers as she slid her arms around his neck, pulling down his head and precluding any further talk.

A week later they were married in London by special licence. It was a very quiet ceremony, Cathy had insisted on that, and Dan had finally given in, with only the bride and groom and the two required witnesses, Holly and a friend of Dan's, Raoul Patterson.

Holly had been madly happy but not particularly surprised when Cathy had broken the news the afternoon Dan had proposed.

'I knew it!' she had declared gleefully, nearly jumping up and down in her excitement. 'The moment I saw the two of you dancing together at Julia and Daddy's party—it was fate.'

Cathy had laughed, half believing that herself and remembering that she had to ring Joe and tell him the good news.

She rang her parents' house a number of times that day and that evening, but could not get through. It had started her worrying about her brother, a nervous state that had not been improved when, telephoning the newspaper where he worked the following morning, she had been informed that he had not been at work for the past week.

In panic she had immediately telephoned Dan, almost crying as she spoke to him. He had come round to Holly's flat within half an hour and before she had known what was happening, she had found herself in his low black car, speeding out of London towards Brighton.

'It's about time I met him,' he had smiled.

She had been amazed at his kindness, his thoughtfulness, the way he had dropped everything to help her.

They found Joe doing some gardening at the house, casually surprised to see them, faintly irritated at Cathy's worried anger.

'I've been trying to reach you!' she had exclaimed, her anger born of relief more than anything else. She had spent an almost sleepless night, imagining him in all kinds of trouble.

'So, now you've reached me, where's the fire?' Joe had asked infuriatingly, carrying on with his task of trimming a privet hedge. Cathy had almost exploded at that. Dan had intervened and taken them all out to lunch, explaining over a delicious meal that he and Cathy were to be married.

Joe had accepted the news easily, obviously impressed by Dan, his attitude for once, respectful. But he had not wanted to come to the wedding, explaining that he would probably be away in Jersey at the time. Cathy had accepted that without question, despite Dan's frown.

They had driven back to London in the late afternoon, and Joe's final words as he kissed Cathy goodbye had been, 'You've landed on your feet there, Cath—he's loaded! Good luck.'

Cathy had shaken her head in despair. Typically Joe, she had thought sadly, wondering how he could be so cynical when he was so young.

On the way back to London Cathy had explained to Dan about her relationship with Joe. They led separate lives, he only ever came to her when he was in trouble and vice versa. It was a

strange but not untypical relationship for brother
and sister, especially in the light of the trauma they
had shared when both had been so young,
unformed and vulnerable.

That evening Dan had given her a ring, a huge
flawless diamond set in gold. Cathy had cried un-
ashamedly, awed by its beauty, shaken by what it
represented. She was engaged to Dan Foreman, the
only man she had ever loved, would ever love, and
her life seemed complete. The rest of the week
hurried by, there was so much to do, including
buying her wedding dress, that Cathy felt she had
barely time to breathe, and in a blinding, terrifying
flash, her wedding day arrived.

She woke early, wondering at the fear in her
stomach, remembering what day it was, as tumultu-
ous emotions dragged sleep from her mind and
body. She jumped out of bed and ran to the
window, pulling up the blind, to see that it was a
clear, bright day. A good omen, she thought nervously, and went to bathe.

She spent ages soaking herself and washing her
hair, and Holly was already up, making coffee and
toast, when Cathy finally entered the kitchen.

'Morning, would you like some toast?' Holly
smiled in greeting.

Cathy shook her head, grimacing. She couldn't
possibly eat, not this morning. 'Just coffee, I
think.'

They sat at the table together, Holly chatting
away merrily as usual, while Cathy sat lost in her
own thoughts, doubts suddenly crowding into her
mind as she realised exactly what she was going to
do today.

It was as though this was the first opportunity
she'd had since Dan had proposed to step back

and actually think objectively about what she had committed herself to. The past week had been one big, hectic rush from dawn to dusk, every single day. There had been no time to think about the larger issues, too many smaller, now seemingly inconsequential things had clouded her vision and filled her time exclusively.

She was frightened. The knowledge hit her like a bomb, her hand gripping her coffee cup so tightly that her knuckles gleamed white. In a couple of hours she would be Dan Foreman's wife, would have vowed to live with him until she died. He was an attractive American, multi-millionaire who would completely change her way of life. I don't know him, she thought hysterically, illogical with fear. Why does he want to marry me?

She stared at Holly, who having given up on conversation with her, was washing up the breakfast dishes, her back turned to Cathy.

Cathy wanted to tell her, confide in her, about the awful thoughts that were running through her mind, but even as she opened her mouth, she knew that the words would not come. She was locked in silence, unable to reveal her terrible doubts.

It was even more of a shock to find that she could not talk to her best and closest friend. What's happening to me? she wondered miserably, staring down at the nervous fingers clenching around the hem of the tablecloth, the gleam of gold and diamond flashing up into her eyes, accusing her somehow.

'You're as white as a sheet,' Holly declared with concern. 'Are you feeling all right?'

This was her chance to confide; Holly was handing it to her on a plate, perhaps sensing something in Cathy.

'Yes, I'm fine, just a little nervous, that's all—a bride's prerogative, I believe.' She heard her forced, cheerful reply with dismay.

'It's only natural, so they tell me,' Holly replied, reassuringly bright.

Afterwards, Cathy often wondered why it had never occurred to her to back out of the wedding, to call it off, cancel at the last minute. It could have been done, even though it would have meant a great deal of unpleasantness and misery. But at the time it never occurred to her, it seemed inevitable and far too late to change anything, irreversible, like the tide.

So instead she went to her bedroom and began to make up her face, skilfully disguising her paleness and her fear with powders and creams. When her face was finished, even she had to admit that she looked beautiful, her eyes huge and mysterious, her complexion faintly flushed with becoming, albeit artificial, colour, her mouth vivid, soft and vulnerable.

Her eyes filled with tears as she thought of her mother, wishing with all her heart that her parents could be there for her wedding. She would have been able to talk to her mother, confide her fears. Her mother would have helped her in this awful dilemma.

Since their death, she had by necessity become too self-sufficient, too withdrawn, finding it impossible to share her problems with others, even close friends, people she trusted, and because she could not talk, she bottled it up inside, letting it grow bigger veering out of proportion. She swallowed back her tears before they fell, fearful of spoiling her careful make-up, and brushed out her hair, tugging the brush through the tousled softness, the pain jerking her back to reality and the present.

Holly helped her thread her loose, silken hair with flowers and helped her dress in the simply cut white silk dress that Cathy had chosen for the ceremony. It was a beautiful dress trimmed with antique lace, with a tight square-necked bodice, long sleeves and a gently flaring skirt that reached just below her knees. As she stepped into her high shoes, she examined herself carefully in the mirror. A tall slender girl in pure white with a cloud of heavy raven hair framing a small face and slim shoulders stared back.

'You look stunning—absolutely gorgeous!' Holly breathed honestly, and Cathy knew it to be the truth. She hardly recognised herself, she looked cool and sophisticated. It's not me at all, she thought in amazement. The real me is inside, crouching in fear and worry, like a child in a dark room.

She spoke none of these thoughts aloud though, merely saying to Holly, 'Will you help me with my jewellery? I've no idea what to choose.'

Finally she decided on a delicately wrought necklace that had belonged to her mother. Fine strands of gold set with milky-white opals, it lay coldly and heavily against the heated skin of her throat. Holly lent her some gold earrings, bright, tiny studs that matched the necklace perfectly.

The final touch was a dab of her favourite perfume on all her pulse spots. She had five minutes before the car was due to arrive and she lit a cigarette with trembling fingers, walking over to the window to look out over the park, her shoulders hunched and tense as she tried to quell her fear.

The ceremony passed quickly, almost before she

noticed, a confused blur. She walked into the register office with Holly, who looked quite beautiful in a pale apricot voile suit, and Dan turned, as if sensing her approach, watching her with dark guarded eyes as she walked towards him, his breath caught by her loveliness.

She stood beside him at last, wondering how on earth her legs were supporting her. They felt like jelly, so very weak. She glanced surreptitiously up at Dan's hard, fleshless profile from beneath her lashes. His face was totally devoid of expression, remote and breathtakingly attractive. He wore a dark, finely pin-striped suit, perfectly and expensively cut to his body. He was formal, alien, and her fear returned in a blinding rush that made her swallow convulsively.

Dan took his vows in a low cool voice, somehow sure, and Cathy felt shaken, close to tears, her own voice small and weak.

He slipped the heavy band of gold on to her finger, publicly branding her as his possession, his wife. Then it was over and Dan was tilting up her chin with gentle fingers, finding her stiff, numb lips in a brief warm kiss. She could not respond to him, her eyes wide, blind as his dark head lowered, instinctively shying away when he slipped his hand beneath her elbow to guide her from the office.

There was a quiet wedding breakfast at the Ritz, and Cathy, pale and silent, watched Holly falling under Dan's powerful, effortless spell, with dull eyes. She managed to smile at Raoul Patterson, a tall, strikingly handsome young man with black hair and flashing dark eyes.

'Dan's a very lucky man,' he remarked in a slow American drawl, his answering smile warm and friendly.

Cathy flushed and sipped her champagne. 'Have you been friends for very long?' she asked, just for the sake of conversation.

'About five years. We work together,' Raoul informed her.

'He's my right-hand man, I'd be lost without him,' Dan cut in, his voice warm and lazy, his eyes resting searchingly on Cathy's suddenly lowered head.

'How nice to be indispensable.' She flashed Raoul a brilliant, empty smile, deliberately evading Dan's probing glance, even though she was tensely aware of it.

'Is there any more of this delicious champagne?' Holly's innocent question broke the moment of tension, as Dan's attention was diverted, unfailingly polite as he refilled Holly's glass.

Raoul was still chatting to her, but Cathy felt very alone, confused and nervous as her glance skittered over Dan, her fingers playing with the unaccustomed heaviness of the thick gold band on her wedding finger. Dan Foreman was now her husband, for better, for worse, until death parted them. It was an awesome thought, one that chilled her as she desperately wondered why she could not recapture her ecstatic happiness of a week before.

She needed to talk to somebody, so standing up, she excused herself and went in search of a telephone, aware of Dan's eyes on her back as she walked from the table. She would telephone Joe, who with his down-to-earth cynicism would help her to put the whole situation into perspective. She hoped.

As the number rang, she remembered him mentioning Jersey, so she rang the newspaper he worked for and after a great deal of fuss, was given the number of a hotel on Jersey where he could be reached. She finally got through and the receptionist tried his room. Cathy tapped her foot impatiently, her desperation building, feeling an embarrassing rush of tears filling her eyes.

Joe was the only family she had in the whole world, it was so unfair that she could not contact him on this, her wedding day, supposedly the most important day of her life. Damn him for being so uncaring sometimes! He should have telephoned her. She was always there when he needed her, why didn't it work the other way round?

The receptionist came back on the line, telling her that Mr Fairfax was not answering, and would she like to leave a message. Cathy declined, misery sweeping over her, and hung up.

She turned on her heel, dabbing ineffectually at her eyes with angry fingers, to find Dan in front of her, leaning indolently against the wall, watching her with veiled eyes.

'Who were you calling?' he asked, his voice curiously tender as he stared into her tear filled eyes.

'Did you follow me?' she asked suspiciously, not answering his question, unable to bear his concern.

'Yes, I followed you. You were edgy, as white as a sheet. I was worried about you,' he replied levelly, ignoring her belligerence.

'I don't want you to worry about me,' she said petulantly, wishing she had the strength to walk away from him but finding that she was rooted to the spot, her heart beating very fast as she stared into his enigmatic green eyes.

'You are my wife.' He said every word slowly, possessively. 'I now have the right to worry about you.'

She stared at him in silence and he leaned over

and touched her face very gently.

'Cathy, I want you to know. ... .'

She did not give him time to finish, suddenly frightened of what he was going to say. She did not want to know.

'I was trying to phone Joe,' she blurted across him. 'He's gone to Jersey. I phoned the hotel, but he was out. . . . I must talk to him!'

Dan nodded, his dark brows meeting in a frown. 'You can call him later. Did you leave a message?'

Cathy shook her head, watching as he picked up the telephone. She gave him the hotel telephone number and listened as he dialled and left a message for Joe on his return.

'He'll call you at my apartment as soon as he gets back,' he told her reassuringly, slipping his arm around her shoulders, propelling her back to their table.

'Dan. . . .' She spoke his name tentatively, not wanting to go back to their friends, finding herself unable to chatter happily as though everything was wonderful.

'What is it?' He stopped patiently and turned her to face him, his eyes warm and dark with emotion as he looked into her small beautiful face.

'Can . . . can we leave now? I feel exhausted,' she said quietly, realising as soon as the words were out that they would be misunderstood.

Dan smiled at her, touching his mouth to her forehead. 'Yes, we can leave immediately.'

They made their excuses and farewells to Holly and Raoul, who understood, then left to drive to Dan's penthouse flat in Mayfair. It had been mutually discussed and agreed that they would spend a night there before flying out to Los Angeles for a few days, where Cathy would be introduced to Dan's family, after which they would travel on to the Bahamas for their honeymoon. Honeymoon. As she leaned back and closed her eyes in Dan's car, Cathy shivered at the implications of that word. She felt a little lightheaded from the amount of champagne she had drunk.

'Cathy, are you all right?' Dan's voice was low, concerned, and she smiled at him stiffly.

'I think I drank too much champagne,' she admitted. Why did her voice sound so strange?

He laughed. 'There's nothing wrong with that,' he teased her gently. She deliberately kept her distance, avoiding any physical contact with him as they took the private lift up to his suite and if Dan noticed her obvious behaviour he did not comment on it.

The apartment itself was enormous, beautifully decorated with huge windows affording panoramic views over the late afternoon city. Cathy wandered around the lounge, a pale slender figure in white silk, touching the books, the sculptures, the polished wood furniture, her feet sinking into the rich Persian carpet. It was an essentially masculine room and she told Dan so.

He shrugged, smiling at her. 'You must change it if you want to,' he teased, though she could see that he meant it.

He showed her the rest of the suite then, the huge modern kitchen, a dining room, another sitting room, a study and numerous bedrooms all with adjoining bathrooms.

Dan told her that now they were married he was considering buying a house in England, probably in the country. Cathy knew as he spoke that he was thinking of her, wanting to give her a home in her own country, but fear was tightening her stomach again and she was noncommittal and uncaring in reply.

She was alone with this unknown man who was her husband, alone in this luxurious, beautiful penthouse suite, and she was afraid. She stood in the lounge again having hardly taken in any of the details of the numerous rooms he had shown her.

'Would you like a drink?' Dan asked quietly, shrugging out of his jacket and pulling off his tie. Cathy stared at him, dry mouthed, watching his swift graceful movements, her eyes fixing on the top button of his waistcoat as she felt him staring back at her. She shook her head, remembering that he was waiting for an answer. 'N . . . no . . . thank you,' she managed, stammering badly.

'Oh, Cathy!' His voice was low, tender as he moved smoothly towards her, standing very close but not touching her. 'What is it, honey?'

His gentleness seemed to crack the block of cold fear inside her and she lifted huge bruised eyes to his lean face.

'You're my husband.' The word was strange, unknown in her mouth. 'Dan, I'm afraid,' she whispered.

He swore softly, reaching for her, pulling her into his arms and holding her tightly. She felt the hard familiar warmth of his body and realised for the first time that day that he was no stranger, no monster to be feared, but a strong, warm man whom she loved. Since waking that morning she had not even thought of him, only herself, and the knowledge shamed her.

She slid her arms around his waist, pressing herself closer to him, hearing the swift intake of his breath, as his own arms tightened. He tilted up her face and she caught the hungry flame in his eyes, a flare of bright, intense light, before he lowered his head and his mouth found hers with fierce necessity.

His kiss was an explosion, tearing through her body, leaving her trembling, yielding within the circle of his arms. She clung to him, feeling the tension in his powerful body as his mouth still moved sensuously, hungrily over hers.

'Make love to me, Dan,' she whispered against his lips, and he groaned softly, sliding his arms beneath her and swinging her up against the hard wall of his chest, carrying her effortlessly into his bedroom and kicking shut the door behind him.

The room was dim in the early evening light and he gently deposited her on the enormous, softly sprung bed, moving beside her immediately, his brown hands reaching for her. He undressed her slowly, expertly, removing the white silk dress and her filmy underwear until she was naked beneath his seeking hands. She flushed hotly under his glittering gaze, unable to move to cover herself, as his eyes moved slowly over her body.

'You're so lovely, Cathy, so very lovely,' he murmured huskily, bending to kiss her again, his mouth urgent and persuasive.

She watched him as he undressed, her attention held on his powerful brown body, the broad hair-roughened chest, the muscled arms, the polished strength of his legs, the potent magnificence of him in the fading light. Then he was beside her again, and their naked bodies came together, fitting so perfectly that they might have been made for each other.

She heard Dan groan as she moved against him teasingly. His mouth found hers again as he began to touch her body, his long hard fingers gently tracing the soft, silken curves from shoulder to thigh, stroking over every inch of her, slowly, unhurriedly, as though the feel of her warm bare skin was enough to drive him beyond control.

Cathy moaned very softly, her body beginning to writhe beneath his slow exploration, her skin heating, bursting into flames wherever he touched her.

His mouth left hers, tenderly kissing her pointed chin, sliding the length of her white throat, his tongue moving against the skin of her shoulder. She arched back her head in surrender as his mouth moved lower to the sensitive slopes of her breasts, her heart beating deeply, hurriedly, her whole body shaking uncontrollably as his tongue teased a hard nipple, his lips finally closing over it, as she dissolved in fierce, hot sensation. She looked down at his proud dark head bent to her breasts and shuddered, her hands tangling in his thick hair to press him closer.

After long, sweet moments, Dan lifted his head, his eyes burning with desire.

'Love me, Catherine,' he ordered softly, and she began to touch him.

His skin was warm and smooth, taut over heavy muscles, his heart hammering as she let her mouth drift down his chest, her tongue flicking against his skin. He began to shake, breathing raggedly, deeply affected by her innocent lovemaking, kissing her, caressing her until she was lost, knowing only her deep need to give herself, to satisfy the hunger she felt in him, to satisfy her own hunger.

At last he moved over her, and she looked up into his face as their bodies became one. He was staring down at her, his eyes flaming, out of control, his skin taut over the hard planes of his face, his mouth compressed, fierce with desire.

Cathy closed her eyes, the image remaining behind her eyelids, crying out his name, her hands clenching cruelly against the smooth skin of his back, as he brought them both to a powerful, all-consuming crescendo of pleasure that finally released and assuaged the tense overpowering hunger between them.

Afterwards, Dan rolled on to his back beside her, pulling her gently into his arms, pressing her head to the sweat-dampened roughness of his chest. Beneath her cheek his heart still pounded, he still breathed heavily, unevenly.

'Dear God, Cathy, nobody else could make me feel like that,' he muttered, holding her tightly, smoothing back her damp, tousled hair.

She laughed shakily, feeling proud, exhausted and fulfilled. 'Dan. . . .' She whispered his name once, against the smoothness of his shoulder, and was asleep.

CHAPTER FIVE

THE following day, as arranged, they flew out to Los Angeles. Before they left Cathy spoke to both Holly and Joe on the telephone. Holly wished her good luck and happiness, not bothering to disguise her envy, and they promised to telephone and write to each other.

Joe also wished her well, and wanted to know why she had telephoned him. It was bad form, he told her, to leave messages at the newspaper and at the hotel, when he was away, working, especially as there was obviously no emergency. Cathy apologised, laughing at him, her fear completely gone after a night in Dan's arms. Although she could have wished for Joe to be a bit nicer to her, there was something distinctly reassuring in his impatience, she thought with a smile as she rang off.

Raoul Patterson accompanied them on the plane, and Cathy found that the more she got to know him the more she liked him. He was charming and intelligent, and his respect and affection for Dan was disarmingly obvious, also extending to herself as Dan's wife.

It was a pleasant journey, relaxed and luxurious, and Cathy was amazed anew by Dan's wealth. To own a plane of one's own, never having to worry about scheduled flights, seemed to her incredible. Dan, however, shrugged it off casually, explaining that it was a necessity. His business ran tightly and his presence was often immediately required at a subsidiary office, thousands of miles away. He needed access to any country in the world, at very short notice, and a private jet was the only feasible answer.

Cathy was impressed, and settled down in her comfortable seat, her face contented as she flicked through the pages of a glossy magazine. She had a lot to learn about her husband's business. Los Angeles was hot and hazy when they arrived at LAX. The formalities were completed with a minimum of fuss. Raoul disappeared almost immediately in an open blue sports car, waving regretfully at Cathy as Dan propelled her towards a long chauffeur-driven limousine which silently transported them to Dan's mansion in the hills. Cathy stared out of the tinted windows at the tall,

gleaming buildings and the dry brown hills, recognising the names on the freeway signposts—
Malibu, Bel Air, Marina del Rey—with excitement
and wonder. Up into the hills the car climbed,
finally slowing before high, automatic gates. Cathy
looked out from the air-conditioned interior of the
car, as the gates opened silently, closing again as
they sailed through down a long, twisting drive
flanked by enormous palm trees, exotic flowers and
incredibly green lawns on which sprinklers played.

When the house came into view she gasped with
delight. An enormous white building, its rows of
windows graced with wrought-iron balconies, a
pillared porch sheltering an arched wooden door,
surrounded by a riot of colourful, flowering vege-
tation. It was beautiful, stark and impressive.

'Do you like it?' Dan asked, watching her carefully, noting her reactions as she stared out of the
window. 'It's lovely!' she whispered in an awed
voice.

'Come inside.' He slid gracefully out of the car,
opening the door for her and taking her hand as
they walked together up the stone steps to the
impressive front door.

Once inside, Dan introduced her to his house-
keeper, Maria Sanchez, a middle-aged Mexican
woman with kind eyes and a plump, happy face. If
Maria was surprised that Dan had brought home a
new wife, she did not show it as she shook hands
and smiled at Cathy. Cathy smiled back, knowing
somehow that they would get on well. She was also
introduced to two enormous Great Dane dogs that
were pathetically happy to greet Dan and bounded
round him, barking madly.

He showed her into a huge lounge with dark
polished floorboards and white walls. In front of

the three arched windows along one wall, stood tall indoor trees in wicker baskets, dappling the strong light that flooded the room.

One wall contained bookshelves from floor to ceiling, holding books, boxes, ornaments and stereo equipment. There was a blue tiled fireplace with another wicker basket, this one filled with logs, on the hearth. Most of the furniture was made of woven cane and elm, with blue cushions, and there were also two blue sofas, the covering material rich cobalt and white, patterned with huge fish. Cathy's eyes skimmed over the low blue-tiled table between the two sofas and the collection of blue and white Chinese porcelain ginger jars, with delight. It was a visually stunning room that incorporated comfort and convenience.

'Would you like a drink?'

'I'd like some coffee, please.' She turned to him, answering his question with a smile.

She curled up on one of the sofas and seconds later Maria Sanchez appeared with a tray that held coffee and a plate of delicious-looking sandwiches.

Cathy poured coffee for them both and handed a cup to Dan. 'It's a beautiful room,' she said enthusiastically, as she sipped her coffee.

He smiled, making her heart turn over. 'As with the apartment in London, you must change whatever you don't like. All the places we will live in, they'll be your homes and I want you to treat them as such,' Dan said seriously, giving her a free rein.

She leaned over and shyly kissed his mouth in gratitude, hearing him catch his breath, his powerful arms coming around her. Suddenly they were clinging together, desire quickening Cathy's blood as Dan's mouth possessed hers with need and hunger, her small hands reaching up to shape his lean, hard-boned face.

A second later a woman's low voice, mockingly amused, broke between them. 'Hi, Dan. You don't waste any time, do you?'

Cathy stiffened in Dan's arms, embarrassed colour washing over her face as she looked up to find herself staring into a pair of blue eyes belonging to the woman she had first seen with Dan at Holly's father's party.

Dan turned his dark head slowly, reluctantly releasing Cathy from his arms.

'Dammit, Natalie, don't you ever knock?' he asked irritably, but he was smiling, and Cathy felt an irrational stab of dislike for the woman who had burst in on them.

She let her eyes wander discreetly over Natalie Benjamin, taking in the other woman's vivid orange dress, long bare legs and the numerous gold bangles that rattled musically on her arm. The red hair was scraped back into a casually stylish pony-tail, the beautiful face was perfectly made up.

Cathy guessed that Natalie was in her early thirties, but she looked younger, and Cathy felt very gauche, childish and rather scruffy by comparison.

Natalie bent down and kissed Dan's cheek with careless intimacy, her tanned hands lingering on his lean face, hardly acknowledging Cathy's presence at all.

'I don't need to knock, you should know that,' she replied coolly. 'Why didn't you tell me you were back?' The complaint was sweetly spoken.

'So how did you find out?' Dan parried, with a veiled smile.

'I bumped into Raoul downtown. . . .'

'Ah, and you wanted a look at Cathy,' Dan

laughed, throwing back his dark head in open amusement.

'It's true then, you are married?' Cathy detected the flat note in the other woman's voice, the flash of fury in the cold blue eyes.

'Yes, it's true. Cathy, I'd like you to meet my cousin and business associate, Natalie Benjamin. Natalie, my wife, Cathy.' His voice was possessive, gentle.

Cathy smiled at Natalie Benjamin. 'Hello, Natalie—can I call you Natalie?' she asked shyly, holding out her hand.

Natalie Benjamins' eyes skimmed over her, openly dismissive. 'Everybody does,' she shrugged, and touched Cathy's hand lightly, very briefly.

She doesn't like me, Cathy thought, and as Natalie looked at Dan, she knew why. The beautiful redhead was in love with Dan, it was burning in her avid blue eyes. Cathy shivered despite the heat, jealousy tearing at her as she poured out more coffee for all of them.

She took the cigarette that Dan offered her and sat silently, shocked by her discovery, outwardly poised and polite, inwardly seething.

'Why all the secrecy?' Natalie asked, sitting down opposite Dan and crossing her long, slim legs rather obviously, Cathy thought. Like Cathy, she accepted a cigarette from Dan, curving a slim hand with long red fingernails over his as he offered her a light.

Dan exhaled smoke from his mouth in a long stream, taking Cathy's hand in his, his fingers moving caressingly over hers.

'No secrecy—we both wanted a quiet wedding.'

Natalie's eyes fixed on their linked hands, her red mouth tightening. 'Does Larry know?'

'Not yet,' Dan said calmly.

'It will be a big surprise.'

'We'll see.' He was implacable. For some reason Natalie was trying to annoy him, but she was getting nowhere, even Cathy could see that.

Finally she got to her feet, politely saying goodbye to Cathy before leaving the room with Dan.

Cathy sat perfectly still in her seat, alone in the beautiful room, staring into space as she thought of Natalie Benjamin. To find that Natalie was in love with Dan was no surprise, but it was rather discomfiting. She had obviously not remembered Cathy from the party, or if she had, she had disguised it very well. Cathy hoped that she would not have to see a lot of Natalie, it was glaringly obvious that they were not going to get on.

Dan re-entered the room, breaking into her reverie. He smiled at her. 'We're invited to dinner at Larry's tonight. Do you want to go, Cathy?'

'Who's Larry?' she wanted to know.

'My father,' he replied, as he moved to sit beside her again.

'In that case, yes, I'd love to go.' She was curious to meet his father, wondering whether or not he would be like Dan.

'Who else will be there?'

'Natalie and Owen—her father, my uncle.'

'Oh.' Cathy's heart sank at the news that Natalie would be there, and all of a sudden she did not want to go. 'Tell me about Natalie,' she said, not looking at him.

Dan shrugged. 'She's my cousin, she works for the company. Her husband works in Saudi Arabia, he works for the company as well. She lives with Larry and Owen—that's about it.'

'She's married?' She spoke half to herself, surprised, very surprised.

'Yes, she's married,' Dan repeated, openly amused. 'Why all the interest in Natalie?'

'No reason,' Cathy muttered quickly, afraid of giving herself away. Did Dan know that Natalie was in love with him? 'Why didn't she go to Saudi Arabia with her husband?'

'She didn't want to, I guess. Her work is here, it means a lot to her.' Dan sounded bored.

'How long has her . . .?' She never finished her question. Dan moved, lightning-fast, and found her mouth with his own, kissing her hungrily until she was breathless, yielding. 'I don't want to talk about Natalie,' he murmured huskily. I don't want to talk at all. I want you.'

Cathy shivered at the raw desire in his voice, wanting him badly, her fingers sliding beneath his shirt to find the muscled flatness of his stomach.

She heard him groan as he lifted her into his arms and carried her from the room, up the huge ornate staircase, to his bed.

A tiny warning voice in her head asked her if it was Natalie who had aroused him so suddenly, so fiercely, and her heart contracted painfully, turning away from that suspicious thought in horror, wondering how she could even have imagined it.

But in the cool darkness of Dan's bedroom he made her forget it, made her forget everything as his hands moved caressingly over her and the heavy weight of his body pressed her into the satin softness of the bed, his mouth warm, hungry, promising heaven.

A long time later she lay beside him, her body

relaxed, languorous, satisfied, her head on his chest, his arms wrapped possessively around her.

'Oh, Cathy, my beautiful Cathy,' he murmured into the tousled softness of her hair.

'What time are we expected for dinner at your father's house?' she asked lazily, stretching against his hard naked body.

'About seven.' Dan's voice was unsteady.

'What time is it now?'

'Six.' He tilted up her chin with gentle fingers and kissed her mouth.

'We'd better get up, we'll be late,' she protested laughingly. 'Dan——'

He silenced her easily, moving swiftly so that she lay beneath him, his body tautening abruptly as he began to touch her again. In the end they were forced to get up, splashing together like children in the enormous tiled shower.

Cathy dried her hair and made up her face, then slipped into a dress of soft bottle green velvet, cut in a slim-fitting classic style. It was one of her favourite dresses and she knew she looked good in it, the colour somehow accentuating her soft brown eyes and pearly skin. She was undecided how to wear her hair, and Dan watched her as he shrugged into his waistcoat, smiling at her pleated forehead.

'Wear it loose,' he suggested softly, bending to press his lips to the nape of her neck.

The decision was made for her and she reached for her hairbrush, surprised when he took it from her, brushing out her hair gently, carefully threading his fingers through its heavy silkiness. 'You look beautiful,' he said, his green eyes truthful, caressing.

They were only ten minutes late arriving at Dan's father's house. As soon as she saw him Cathy knew who he was. He was tall, his ageing body still powerful, his hair thick like Dan's, but iron-grey, with the same grey-green eyes and hard-boned face.

'You must be Cathy.' He greeted her with a warm smile, kissing both her cheeks. 'Natalie has told me all about you, and now that I've seen you I can understand why my son wanted to keep you to himself.'

'I'm very pleased to meet you, Mr Foreman,' Cathy smiled, liking him immediately, slightly flushed from his compliments.

'Larry—I insist.' His voice had the same low drawl as Dan's.

She watched as father and son greeted each other. There was a strong, easy affection between them, and something else, which she recognised as true friendship.

They walked through the house on to a large, softly-lit patio, surrounding a calm blue swimming pool. Natalie and her father sat round a long cane table, both getting to their feet as the guests appeared. Cathy was introduced to Owen Foreman—he too bore a family resemblance to Dan, and Natalie, her eyes fixed on Cathy's husband, offered drinks, her long white caftan and burnished hair making Cathy feel dull and dowdy in her dark velvet.

It was a pleasant evening, spiced with an air of celebration and with the exception of Natalie, Cathy found it easy to get on with Dan's family. The food was mouthwatering and it was good to eat in the open air, under a warm, clear, star-sprinkled sky. Over coffee as they all sat back replete, Cathy was suddenly shocked to hear Natalie say, 'If you have nothing planned for tomorrow,

Cathy, perhaps we could meet for lunch and I can show you the town. I'm sure you want to do some shopping before you leave for the Bahamas.'

It was probably a veiled insult about her clothes, but Cathy was too surprised at the sweetly spoken invitation to do more than make a mental note of it. Her eyes instinctively sought Dan's, wondering what to do.

'I'm sure Dan won't mind me stealing you away for an hour or two.' Natalie had caught Cathy's nervous action, picking up on it immediately.

Dan smiled at Cathy, his eyes lazy, shadowed with emotion. 'I won't mind so long as it's only for an hour or two.'

'Sounds like a good idea to me,' Larry cut in, and Cathy could see that he was trying to foster friendship between herself and Natalie, trying to make her part of the family.

She wanted to refuse, suspicious of Natalie's motives, but it was impossible; Natalie had cleverly outmanoeuvred her.

'Yes, that sounds lovely,' she agreed, trying to inject some enthusiasm into her voice. She did not miss the cold triumph in Natalie's eyes, and it worried her.

'I'll pick you up at noon,' the other woman said lightly, turning her attention back to Dan almost immediately.

It was well after midnight when they left and Cathy closed her eyes, leaning her head against Dan's shoulder as they drove home. She felt utterly weary; the plane journey, the difference in time zones, the nervous strain of meeting Dan's family for the first time and the wine at dinner had left her suddenly weak and exhausted. She stumbled, almost falling as she got out of the car, her eyes dazed, not focussing, and Dan lifted her into his arms, concern tightening his mouth as he carried her inside. She was asleep before they reached the bedroom, totally unaware of him as he put her to bed, unaware that he watched her sleeping for long minutes before sliding in beside her and pulling her into the strong protective circle of his arms, letting sleep finally claim him.

Cathy was ready early the following day for her lunch appointment with Natalie. The other girl arrived exactly at noon, speeding up the long drive in an open-topped white sports car.

She was cool but polite, her blue eyes flicking disdainfully over Cathy's neat hair, pale mauve sundress and long bare legs.

As they drove down the hill, Cathy was still trying to quell her suspicions. Perhaps Natalie did not have any ulterior motive for inviting her out shopping, perhaps she really did want to make a friend out of Dan's wife. As she thought of Dan Cathy's face softened, her lips curving in a soft smile as she remembered his mouth, warm and insistent, waking her early that morning, his body hard and hungry, his hands gentle.

She loved him so completely, eagerly gave everything of herself to him, flushing now as she remembered the primitive abandon of her response to his lovemaking.

Natalie caught that dreamy flush as they turned a corner and her mouth hardened, although she remained silent.

They stopped at Rodeo Drive in Beverly Hills. The shops were wonderful there, but a lot of the fun of shopping was taken away for Cathy as she strolled round with Natalie. It was rather like shopping with one's schoolteacher, she thought wryly. Natalie was polite, obviously in charge and faintly frosty. However, she made the best of it, ignoring the other girl's little icy remarks for most of the time, and buying some swimwear and two thin, beautifully patterned cotton dresses for her honeymoon. That morning Dan had pushed what seemed like an enormous amount of money into her hand, for this shopping expedition.

Cathy had looked at it in amazement for a moment. 'I can't take this,' she had said firmly, on finding her voice.

'Why not?' Dan had smiled indulgently.

'It's far too much and . . . and I can't take your money,' she had stammered.

'Cathy, you're my wife, what's mine is yours, and you'll need some money if you're going shopping with Natalie.'

'It's too much,' she had repeated, staring at him wide-eyed.

'I have plenty of money,' he had assured her with gentle patience. 'Take it.'

So finally she had, but she had no intention of spending it all. By lunchtime she had added to her parcels, having bought two evening dresses, one in gold and one in black satin, two pairs of high-heeled sandals and some underwear. She had been wildly extravagant, she thought ruefully, as they took the main road to a small exclusive restaurant well known to Natalie, but at least she would not need any new clothes for ages and ages to come.

She suddenly felt very happy. She liked Los Angeles, she decided, it seemed a good place to live, although it wouldn't have mattered where she lived as long as she was with Dan. Once seated at their table, as they both tucked into seafood starter dishes, Natalie suddenly said, 'You're in love with him, aren't you?' Her voice was faintly sarcastic.

Cathy was startled by her directness. I'm not the only one, she thought silently. 'Yes, I love Dan,' she said calmly. 'And you, Natalie—do you love your husband?' She knew she was being rather rude, but she also knew that if she let Natalie get the better of her now the other girl would walk all over her in the future.

'No.' Again Natalie was startlingly direct. And honest, Cathy thought grudgingly. 'Dick and I have a . . . mutual arrangement.'

That did not explain anything to Cathy. 'He's in Saudi Arabia, isn't he?' she asked politely, finding it very difficult to mask her uneasiness.

'I believe so,' Natalie replied with a smug, uncaring smile. 'Dan was such an angel about getting rid of him, and of course he was in the perfect position to do it for me without arousing suspicion.'

'You wanted your husband to go away?' Cathy's careful mask slipped for a second and there was an inexplicable pain around her heart as the knowledge sank in that Dan had arranged for Natalie's husband to be sent abroad on company business.

'Of course I did.' Natalie was derisive. 'And as young as you are, it should be obvious to you exactly what I want.'

Cathy put her fork down carefully, unable to take another mouthful of food, feeling rather sick but determined not to let Natalie see that. What was happening here?

'Dan,' she said painfully, very quietly.

Natalie laughed. 'I told him you're not as naïve as you look!'

Cathy swallowed convulsively. So Dan had discussed her with Natalie. The knowledge hurt her beyond words. It was a betrayal, a totally un-expected betrayal, if it was true.

'I thought you and I ought to get together as soon as possible,' Natalie continued relentlessly, pressing her advantage. 'Hence this little shopping trip, so that we can come to some agreement right from the start. It will be so much easier that way.'

She seemed very keen on sorting things out, mutual arrangements, early agreements. First her unwanted husband and now Cathy herself.

'I'm afraid I don't know what you're getting at,' Cathy said stiffly, unable to meet Natalie's eyes. There would be amusement and triumph in the blue depths and Cathy suddenly felt very unsure of herself, of Dan, of her new life here in Los Angeles.

'Come now, you're not unaware of Dan's reasons for marrying you,' Natalie said casually.

They might have been discussing clothes, recipes, anything unimportant. It was totally unreal, and all Cathy's fears of two days before crowded back into her confused mind, knocking the ground from beneath her feet. It seemed that she *was* unaware of Dan's reasons for marrying her, but she knew with sickening certainty that Natalie was about to enlighten her.

'You tell me,' she managed with just a touch of defiance.

'He hasn't discussed it with you yet?' It was Natalie's master stroke. This young, pathetically innocent girl was going to be very, very easy. Dan would be sorry, she would make damned sure of that! She raised her thin, perfectly curved eyebrows in surprise. 'Perhaps he's had other things on his mind.' The implication was obvious.

Cathy frowned, a terrible sense of foreboding washing over her. She had to know what Natalie was hinting at. 'Perhaps you should tell me exactly what you're talking about. I don't want any games, Natalie, just the facts.' Her voice was level and she looked the other woman straight in the eye. She reached into her handbag and drew out her cigarettes, lighting one with hands that only shook a little.

'Well, if that's what you want——' Natalie said delicately.

'It's what I want,' Cathy repeated firmly.

'Yes, you do have a right to know, I suppose. I do feel rather angry with Dan for leaving it up to me, though.' Natalie shrugged. 'I was married very young—Dick is a good deal older than myself. Oh, I thought I was in love with him, but what does one know of love at eighteen?' It was a calculated dig and although it hurt, Cathy did not allow it to register on her pale face.

'Go on,' she prompted, tightly.

'I hadn't seen Dan for years. We lived in Chicago then, and he was away travelling the world with Tom, but when we met up again. . . .' Natalie paused, moving her shoulders in an all-encompassing, meaningful shrug. 'Well, I'm sure you don't want to hear *all* the finer details.' Her eyes told Cathy in no uncertain terms that she and Dan had become lovers, had remained lovers all these years.

'Why didn't you divorce your husband and marry Dan, if what you say is true?' Cathy demanded, cold with anger and jealousy, uncertain whether or not to believe Natalie but hating her either way.

'It wasn't possible, my dear, it still isn't. Apart from the fact that Dick won't give me a divorce, I have to think of my father. My mother was a Catholic, you see, a very strict Catholic, and when

they married, my father also became a Catholic—
and of course they brought me up as one too. Since
her death he's become even more devout, religion
is the cornerstone of his life now, and as I'm sure
you know, the Catholic church does not recognise
divorce. But even more important is the fact that
Papa has a heart condition, and I shudder to think
what it would do to him if I divorced Dick to marry
Dan. He couldn't take it, it would probably kill
him,' she finished succinctly.

Cathy was silent, drawing deeply on her cigarette, feeling sorry for Owen Foreman. It was difficult to believe that Natalie was so concerned about
her father's wellbeing. No, that was unfair. She
might hate Natalie, but she did not really know
her, and whatever her bad points, she had seen
Natalie's love for Owen, the previous evening, and
it had been obvious that they were very close.

'That doesn't explain why Dan married me,' she
said quietly.

Natalie smiled, a thin, malicious, genuinely
amused smile. 'A man in Dan's position needs a
wife—the longer you live here, the more you'll
realise that. Somebody to entertain his clients,
proof of his stability and reliability—you know the
sort of thing. Any scandal could harm the company, especially when he has such lucrative contracts with a number of Muslim states. Scandal
could also damage Larry—politics is another field
where stability is important. It was a cover, my
dear, it put the family's mind at rest, especially
Papa's, who I think might have been getting a little
suspicious, and it helped business. Dan is a very
clever man, killing so many birds with one stone.
Mind you, intelligence is only one of his many
talents, as I'm sure you know. Tell me, how do you

find him as a lover? I imagine. . . .'

'*Stop it!*' Cathy jumped to her feet, feeling physically sick at the avid curiosity in Natalie's eyes. 'I don't believe a *word* you've said to me! You're a bitch and a liar!' she almost shouted, uncaring that heads were turning their way, curious eyes and ears trying to catch what was going on at their table, objectively enjoying the angry scene. She snatched up her handbag and ran from the restaurant, her head spinning round and round, unbearably confused and deathly cold inside.

CHAPTER SIX

SHE ran blindly on to the sunny street and straight into somebody. Strong arms steadied her and she looked up, an apology hovering on her lips, to find herself staring into the face of Raoul Patterson. Somehow she was not surprised.

'Hey, Cathy, are you okay?' His dark eyes were concerned, his hands dropping from her arms. It took all her self-control to swallow back her tears and icy misery and smile at him.

'Hello, Raoul, I'm fine, I wasn't looking where I was going—sorry.'

He was easily convinced and they strolled along chatting together for a while, Cathy changing her direction to suit his as she was going nowhere in particular, only away from Natalie.

'Raoul, are you very busy?' she asked as they crossed the noisy main road.

'No, why, what can I do for you?' he questioned obligingly.

'I don't like to ask, but could you give me a lift home?' She knew she was asking a lot, but she did not want to be alone, not just yet.

'I'd be glad to,' Raoul replied graciously, and ten minutes later his car was speeding through the hills towards Dan's home.

Cathy turned in her seat and asked Raoul, 'Natalie works with you doesn't she? How do you get on with her?' She did not imagine the faint flush that stole across his cheekbones.

'Fine—we get on fine,' he replied, gruff and vague, not looking at her, obviously embarrassed.

'And Dan, how does he get on with her?' Cathy probed, driven by something relentless and desperate, wondering at Raoul's acute discomfort at the mention of Natalie's name.

'Look, Cathy, if—well, if you don't mind I'd rather not talk about Natalie. I'm sorry.'

A cold hand squeezed her heart. In her confused state his embarrassed, quietly spoken words seemed to lend truth to what Natalie had said. Her affair with Dan must be common knowledge. Raoul obviously knew about it, but he was Dan's friend and his affection and respect for her husband silenced him. She had put this helpful and likeable young man in an impossible position, and she suddenly felt ashamed of herself. She could not expect him to betray Dan, even though he had told her what she needed to know by his silence, by his embarrassment.

She touched his arm. 'No, I'm sorry. Let's forget it, shall we? I hope we're going to be friends, and I don't want anything to spoil that.'

He smiled at her and she could see the relief in his eyes. 'I know we're going to be friends,' he said brightly.

He dropped her at the gates, but refused to come in, saying that he had to get back to work. Cathy thanked him for the lift and waved goodbye, still feeling terribly guilty about using him. She had been left with no choice, though. Natalie's story had left her with doubts that Raoul had unwittingly proved horribly true, it seemed to her at that moment.

She walked slowly up the drive wondering why she felt so calm, so cold. She had just found out that her marriage was a fake, that Dan did not love her, but was merely using her to cover up his affair with his cousin. She lifted her hand to her face and found it soaked with tears. She was not calm at all, she realised hysterically.

To her relief the house was deserted, with no sign of Dan or Maria. There was a note for her in Dan's strong handwriting, propped up on a table in the massive hall, but she did not read it, merely glanced at it through dull tearful eyes and walked past, upstairs to the bedroom, where she flung herself on the bed and cried as though her heart was broken.

The telephone rang while she lay there, but she did not answer it, knowing that it was Dan. With her self-confidence deeply shaken she went over and over what Natalie had said and the way that Raoul by his silence had somehow proved her story. If she had wondered why Dan had wanted to marry her, wondered how she could possibly have held his attention for so long, she now knew the truth. He had known that she loved him—it must have been very obvious to a man of his experience—and he had used that love ruthlessly, marrying her, knowing that she would never question him, while openly carrying on an affair with a woman he had loved for years.

She thought of the nights she had spent in his arms, his hungry, passionate lovemaking, and humiliation and pain so strong, so physical that it made her gasp, ran through her. Dan had used her body as well. Natalie knew that and did not seem to care. Natalie's love for him must be almost as strong as her own, Cathy thought in anguish.

Dan was ruthless and cold. She did not know him at all—how could she? She had known him for such a short time. Her love had blinded her, letting her believe that he loved her in return, when all the time, she now realised, some small part of her had always doubted her ability to inspire love in a man like Dan. She should have listened to that sane, sensible part of her brain, instead of pushing her doubts aside and marrying him. She loved him even now. It seemed that nothing could destroy that love, she would always love him, and the knowledge made her bitter with misery.

What would she do? She rolled on to her back, staring up at the ceiling as the telephone at the bedside started to ring again. She could not stay with him, that was certain, she would not stay to be used by a man who did not love her. He desired her now—an added bonus for him, she supposed cynically, but when he tired of her as he surely would, she would be left with nothing but her knowledge of the situation. It would destroy her.

She would go back to England. It was her only choice, and besides, it did not matter what she did as long as she was away from Dan. She lay perfectly still on the bed for over an hour, wrestling with her thoughts and her dreadful hurt. It never occurred to her to question the truth of what

Natalie had told her, especially not after speaking to Raoul. Natalie was older, had not disguised her feelings for Dan, and Cathy's self-doubt, her deeply rooted lack of self-confidence had eaten away all her trust in Dan, and she was too young, too inexperienced and too hurt, to see any different reality in the situation. She was alone in an alien country, married for less than a week, to a man who was so complicated and so far removed from all the other men she had known that it was easy to believe that she did not know him.

Finally she sat up on the bed and lit a cigarette. She had cried herself dry, empty, and she was surprised at how strong she felt. She was thinking clearly, coldly, as though she had somehow managed to detach herself from the situation she found herself in. She walked over to the window and looking out saw Dan's car coming up the drive. She stared at it numbly, wondering what on earth she would say to him when he came in. Then as the car drew nearer, she saw that he was not alone. Natalie was in the passenger seat, and anger swept over her. Had Natalie told Dan of their little chat over lunch, reassured him that now Cathy had been put in the picture and knew the facts, there was no further need to hide their affair? Even as she watched from the upstairs window, the car pulled to a halt and Natalie went into Dan's arms.

Cathy turned away, stricken, amazed at their callous blatancy. She sat down on the edge of the bed again because her legs would not hold her up and she was shaking violently from head to foot. Five minutes later Dan appeared in front of her. She did not look up at him.

'Cathy, how long have you been home? Why didn't you answer the phone?' There was a sharp edge to his voice. 'Why didn't you read the note I left?'

She finally looked up at him, her heart constricting with love and pain. He looked worried, tired, his green eyes shadowed and incredibly weary.

'Why are you angry with me?' she asked dully, surprised to find that she could talk to him without shouting and screaming and accusing him.

He sighed, raking a hand through his dark hair. 'I'm not angry with you,' he said gently.

He reached out to touch her face, but she jerked away, not wanting him near her. He did not seem to notice, merely stared down into her pale face. 'I was worried about you. I thought you were with Natalie, but she told me that you'd left, so I called here, but there was no answer.' Cathy was silent, unable to believe that he was so worried about her. There had to be something else.

'What's happened?' she asked quietly.

'It's Owen—he's had a massive heart attack, and they can't say whether or not he'll pull through,' Dan said wearily.

Cathy sat bolt upright, staring at him, shocked by the news, sympathy filling her eyes. 'Oh, Dan, I'm so sorry. Is there anything I can do?'

'It's no surprise,' Dan said almost to himself. 'He's had a bad heart for years, the doctors were always warning him. . . .' He paused, his eyes devouring the love and sympathy he saw in her face. 'No, there's nothing you can do, nothing anybody can do. Natalie is in the car, she's dreadfully upset, I have to run her back to Larry's. I had to check that you were all right first. I'll be back as soon as I can.'

Then he was gone, and Cathy lit another cigarette without noticing and smoked it absently. One thought dominated her mind: Natalie had not been lying about Owen's health. Natalie had been in Dan's arms in the car. I must get away from here as soon as possible, she thought fiercely.

As it turned out she saw hardly anything of Dan over the next few days. Owen's condition was critical, Natalie had called a priest to his bedside and the family spent most of the time at the hospital. Cathy went with Dan once or twice, but the endless waiting, the terrible strain she saw in Dan and Larry, and close contact with Natalie, was more than she could take. Dan, unable to bear her obvious distress, urged her to stay at home, which she finally agreed to do.

Their honeymoon had been postponed until Owen's condition changed one way or the other. Cathy had pushed for this and had been profoundly thankful when Dan agreed. During the long days and nights that Dan spent with Larry and Natalie at the hospital, she began to formulate her plan for leaving him.

The atmosphere in the house changed; both were tense and exhausted, their conversation minimal on the brief occasions when they were together, due to the terrible strain on both of them, but Dan was always gentle with her, apologising for his behaviour, his absence, the postponement of their honeymoon.

He talked a lot about Owen, and Cathy learned how much he cared for his uncle, her heart bled to see him so worried, so tired.

At night when he came home late, she always pretended to be asleep, knowing that she would be unable to bear it if he tried to make love to her. She would listen to him moving quietly, carefully so as not to wake her and she knew as he lay beside her that, like her, he did not sleep.

One night, three days after Owen's attack, she felt him gently touch her arm as she lay with her back to him, silent and very still. 'Cathy, are you asleep?' His voice was low, strained, and she could not ignore him.

'What is it?' she asked, turning over, cursing herself for her own weakness.

'Owen's condition worsened tonight. The doctors don't hold out much hope for him now,' he revealed flatly, his warm breath fanning her cheek.

Cathy sighed, as she heard the pain in his voice, loving him desperately. Despite herself she reached out and touched his lean face.

'Dan, my love, I'm so sorry, I wish there was something I could do,' she whispered tenderly, at the mercy of her deep love for him. For some reason, at that moment it did not matter that he loved Natalie, only that he was turning to her in the dim light, needing her.

'Hold me, Cathy, for God's sake hold me,' he whispered deeply. She laid her arms around his waist, automatically obeying him, hurting inside as his arms slid around her, tightening desperately around her slender body as though he would never let her go. They lay together in the soft, warm, nearly dawn light, both deriving comfort from the close physical contact. Cathy shut her eyes, torn by her conflicting emotions. It was good to be so close to him. Gradually his breathing became slower, steadier, and she realised that he was asleep. He had not slept for days, he must have been exhausted. She opened her eyes again and looked into his face, memorising every feature, every strong line, with an intensity that shocked her, until, surprising herself, she too fell asleep.

Two days later, news came that Owen had passed the worst and had even improved very slightly. After all, it now seemed certain that he was not going to die. Larry began to mention their honeymoon and Cathy knew that the time was fast approaching when she would have to confront Dan and tell him that she was leaving.

It was the most miserable time of her life; nothing held any joy for her and she would wake every morning feeling lethargic and depressed, knowing that the day ahead would be one long grinding struggle.

The situation between her and Dan had not improved. He had noticed her intense withdrawal, the way she flinched away from any physical contact with him. He had tried to talk to her, coax her from her misery, but she had either been silently unco-operative or downright belligerent. In the end, he too had become remote, never touching her, always polite, knowing that the first move would have to come from her.

One morning, she showered and dressed without interest, sipping her coffee and smoking heavily, knowing with an inner certainty that today was the day. Dan was downstairs, talking with Raoul who had arrived early because of a business crisis. She would go down and talk to him as soon as Raoul left.

She walked slowly down the main staircase, counting the steps, not feeling at all nervous, but cold and rather dead inside. As she reached the bottom, she could hear the two men talking, laughing together through the open door. She sat on the stairs, not wanting to intrude, idly listening to their conversation and enjoying the sound of Dan's low, cool voice. Suddenly she caught Dick's name in the conversation. They were talking about Natalie's husband, and she began to listen carefully.

'You want me to contact Dick today, then,' Raoul was saying.

'As soon as possible,' Dan replied in clipped tones. Raoul said something then that Cathy did not catch and both men laughed. 'I admit it, it was one of the best things I ever did, sending Dick out there,' Dan said, still laughing.

'Natalie approves too,' Raoul added.

'Not as much as you,' came the dry reply.

The conversation veered on to another topic then and Cathy ceased to listen. Dan had just incriminated himself, admitting the truth of what Natalie had told her. Not that Cathy needed any more convincing, it all seemed beyond doubt as she lay in the darkness night after night, trying to work things out.

Raoul was leaving and she hurriedly got to her feet, pretending that she had just that minute come downstairs. He smiled at her.

'Hello, how are you?'

'Hello, Raoul, I'm well, thank you. And you?'

'Working hard,' he said, raising his eyebrows in mock despair at her.

Cathy strolled into the blue and white sitting room to wait for Dan. She would be sorry to leave this house, she had felt at home here right from the beginning.

She flicked back her hair and smoothed down the yellow cotton of her dress, watching Dan as he came back into the room, dark brows frowning as he concentrated on the sheaf of papers in his hand, not noticing her for a second.

He looked devastatingly attractive in tight denim

jeans and a pale cotton shirt, open low at the neck, and she felt the damnable weakness in her stomach, the magnetic potency of his attraction, drawing her against her will.

He looked up then and saw her, smiling warily. They had argued bitterly the night before and he was obviously surprised to see her. She had not disguised her coldness, her aversion to being alone with him. Dan had been furiously angry, but remotely polite and very far away. They both knew now that something was seriously wrong between them.

He indicated a tray of coffee on one of the tiled tables. 'Maria has just brought that up. Would you like a cup?' His voice was cool and impersonal. Cathy nodded, not trusting her voice, and moved stiffly over to the table to pour some out.

She did not want any coffee, of course, but she was finding this so difficult that she was thankful for the small diversion. She poured out two cups and handed one to Dan. He sat down opposite her, staring at her, noting the dark circles beneath her eyes, the pallor of her skin, his own eyes softening. Nervously Cathy took a sip of her coffee; it was much too hot and scalded her mouth. She put the cup down carefully, willing her hands not to shake. This was ridiculous, she *had* to get it over with.

'Dan, I . . . I want to talk to you,' she began in a small voice.

'Talk, I'm listening,' he replied expressionlessly.

She took a deep breath. 'I want to go back to England.' Incredibly her voice was level, almost calm.

Dan stiffened imperceptibly. 'For how long?'

'For good. I . . . I don't want to live with you

any more,' she faltered painfully, not knowing how she could do this.

'Why, Cathy?' he demanded flatly, his green eyes totally blank, his mouth furiously angry, but totally in control of himself, as always.

She licked her lips nervously. During her long sleepless nights she had planned this conversation and what lies she would tell to force him to let her go.

'I don't love you,' she said quietly, anguish squeezing her heart as she lied to him. 'And I can't live with you——'

Dan got to his feet angrily, gracefully, hauling her off the couch, his hands hurting her, bruising her shoulders and arms. 'You little bitch,' he said, too softly, his mouth twisting cynically as he stared down into her fearful brown eyes.

'Let me go,' she whispered, but he only laughed, a harsh, bitter noise that was without humour.

'Why the hell should I?' he taunted. 'I've taken your coldness for too damned long!' He lowered his dark head, his mouth finding hers with brutal expertise, kissing her angrily, hurting her. She did not move, did not respond, but remained totally passive beneath the fierce assault of his mouth. Then his kiss suddenly changed, becoming deep, persuasive and gentle, coaxing a response from her that she would rather have died than shown. His hands became gentle too, moving to tangle in her hair, to touch her white throat, as he parted her lips. She loved him, she could not deny him, but she was achingly aware of what would happen if she gave in to him. Unable to stop them, her tears fell slowly, soaking her face.

Tasting their saltiness against his lips, Dan abruptly released her, swearing violently beneath his breath and breathing deeply as he moved away.

'Please let me go,' Cathy begged him, wiping her tears away with shaking hands.

'You haven't given me one good reason why I should,' he said coldly, turning to face her, still angry, the eyes that flicked over her still totally blank.

'There's somebody else.' It was her final desperate lie. If he did not let her go, he would destroy her. She had to get away.

'In England?' His voice was harsh, his face twisted with what she might have thought was pain if she had not known that he did not love her, that he loved Natalie.

'Yes—I've had a letter from him, you gave it to me yesterday at breakfast, remember?' she asked desperately, unable to meet his eyes. She knew that he would remember the brightly coloured airmail envelope. It had been from Joe but she used it ruthlessly now to lend credence to her lie.

'I see.' Dan walked over to the window, turning his back so that she could not see his face. She stared at his powerful body, at his proud dark head. This was the worst, most despicable thing she had ever done, and she hated herself.

'Do you love him, Cathy?' she heard the bitterness in his cold voice.

'Yes . . .' she got out chokingly, aware that she could not bear much more of this. 'Dan. . . .'

'Go—as soon as you like. As far as I'm concerned you're free.' He did not turn round. It was what she had wanted to hear, but instead of relief, she felt only agony. 'Dan. . . .'

'Just go. Now,' he cut in expressionlessly, and she turned and fled the room.

Two days later she was back in the grey cold of England. She had not seen Dan after that dreadful conversation.

From the bedroom where she had rushed in tears, she had heard him leave, the tyres of his car squealing protestingly down the drive. He had not come back and she imagined he had gone to Natalie. She had packed all her things that afternoon, not caring whether she took them with her or not, but because it gave her something to do. She felt as though she wanted to die as she sat on the bed all through the night, smoking incessantly, staring into the darkness and wondering where Dan was.

She even had second thoughts about her decision to leave, although it was too late to change anything. If she stayed, pretending that she did not know about Natalie and Dan. . . . No, it would not have worked. She could not have lived with him, let him make love to her, knowing that he was probably thinking of Natalie. She had made the right decision, she supposed, weary with sadness. She had not hurt Dan, she could not hurt him, he was merely angry because she had wrecked his careful plan. She prayed that she could hate him for what he had done, but found that she couldn't. She loved him just as deeply as she always had. Damn him!

These thoughts swirled round in her head all night, running in circles, getting nowhere and only hurting her more. Finally, when dawn broke and Dan had still not returned she took a taxi to the airport and the first flight back to England. Unable to face anybody, she stayed alone and anonymous in a London hotel for a fortnight while she pulled herself together.

She wrapped her heart in cold ice, managed to kill all her outward feelings so that she could face people without breaking down. It was a long, painful haul, all the more difficult because she found it terribly pointless. She had no desire to start again, to build a new life without Dan. He was everything she wanted, and he was totally beyond reach. Without him she was empty, she had nothing at all.

Months gradually passed and she heard nothing from him, except for a letter sent through her bank from his Los Angeles lawyers, offering her a monthly sum of money to live on and enclosing a legal agreement. She read the letter over and over again, amazed at his generosity, alternating between tears of sadness and of anger.

She finally wrote back to the lawyers, stating in no uncertain terms that she wanted no money from Dan, not ever. It was the final break from him, somehow, the termination of their relationship. She read about him in the newspapers, of course, always knowing when he was in England, reading avidly any scrap of information about him, anxious to know how he was, what he was doing.

On leaving the hotel in London she moved back into her parents' house in Brighton with Joe. But she found that their relationship was changed. She needed privacy now, and they soon began to grate on each other's nerves, he becoming impatient with her misery, she becoming angry with his careless cynicism. After a month or two of sheer hell, it was mutually agreed between them to sell their parents' house. They both needed somewhere to live, and as they found that they could not live together any more, it seemed the only solution.

As soon as the deal went through Cathy bought

her stone cottage near the beach and somehow
began to get her life in order again. She was glad
to be living alone. Her brief marriage to Dan had
changed her a lot, so her friends told her, and she
sometimes found it strangely difficult to recognise
herself. She was almost a different person, quieter,
more withdrawn, but still deeply in love with Dan.

She began to do some work for friends and
gradually built up a small business for herself. Her
success was due to her hard work, she would work
twenty-four hours a day if necessary—she had
nothing else to fill her time.

She daily expected some communication from
Dan, informing her that he wanted a divorce, but
none came. Natalie would never be free to marry,
and as time went by she supposed that he did not
really need a divorce.

She met Greg Calvert through one of her friends,
also a client. She was aware that he was attracted
to her and subsequently refused all of his invita-
tions. She liked him well enough, but she certainly
had no intention of getting involved with him. Tall
and blond, he was an architect—a good one. He
was quiet and polite, a thoroughly nice person, and
in the end, after months of gentle pestering, Cathy
agreed to have dinner with him. On that first evening, she noticed him glancing frequently at her
wedding ring, which she still wore, and briefly explained to him that she was separated from her
husband, unaware that her anguished eyes and
vulnerable mouth told him the whole story.

Greg was easy, amusing and uncomplicated
company and he did not try to push her into anything beyond the occasional evening out. He had
never even kissed her, sensing that it would spoil
the slowly growing friendship between them. Cathy

was glad that he understood the situation. She felt
sure that she would never be able to let a man
touch her again. Dan had been her one and only
lover.

Slowly her mind drifted back to the present. The
train was fast approaching London and Dan. She
lit a cigarette. She had only just managed to get
herself on her feet again, it had taken eighteen
difficult months and now it could all be destroyed
in one afternoon. But mixed with her fear of seeing
her husband again was a strange pleasure. In some
ways it was what she had been aching for ever since
leaving Los Angeles—to see him again, to be able
to look at him, to talk to him. Oh God, how I love
him, she thought, knowing a bitter self-contempt.
He hates me, has no desire to see me again, and
here I am, longing to be in the same room as him
for a few minutes.

She still despised herself for the lies she had told
him. Her only excuse was that she had been so
young, so easily influenced, she'd had no idea how
to cope with a husband who did not love her. Now
she would act differently. She would not lie to him;
pride was worth nothing when it left you alone,
deeply in love with a man who despised you for
what he thought you were.

She felt sure that Dan would not loan her the
money for Joe. Why should he? He owed her
nothing. But if she did not get the money from
Dan, there was nothing she could do for Joe, and
she did not dare to think what would happen to
him.

She sighed heavily and stubbed out her cigarette
as the train pulled slowly and noisily into the
station. She took a taxi to her client's address and

spent an hour or so outlining the details of her ideas to her. Her mind was not on the job, though, and she left as soon as possible. It had been a silly idea to think that she could possibly do any work when she had this interview with Dan hanging over her head like a threatening black cloud.

She went to a café and drank coffee, glancing at her watch every five minutes as two-thirty loomed inexorably nearer and nearer. Finally, far too soon, it was time to make her way to Foreman Incorporated, so she hailed a taxi and as it sped through the London streets, she felt her hands clenching into fists, the knuckles gleaming white with strain.

Her stomach was in turmoil, her mouth dry and her heart beating far too fast as the taxi drew up outside the huge modern office block. It was two-twenty-five.

CHAPTER SEVEN

CATHY stepped through the automatic doors quickly, fearing that if she did not go in immediately she never would. Her feet sank into deeply-piled carpet as she made her way over to the reception desk. She informed the immaculately groomed young woman there of her appointment and was requested to wait, the young woman indicating a comfortable leather sofa.

Thanking her, Cathy sat down, her nerves still fluttering badly in her stomach. How long would Dan keep her waiting? she wondered, as she watched her hands nervously pleating the cool green tweed of her skirt. Not long, obviously, because a second later a tall attractive blonde woman in a beautifully cut blue suit arrived in front of her.

'Mrs Foreman? I'm Helen Gowers—if you'll follow me, Mr Foreman will see you now.'

Cathy smiled and got to her feet, almost amused at the interest in Helen Gowers' eyes. She followed Dan's secretary into the lift that silently carried them to the top of the building. As they stood together in the small bright lift, Cathy knew that the other woman was surreptitiously watching her, assessing her clothes, her hair, her looks, and she wondered what Helen Gowers knew of her. Did Dan ever talk about her? She found the idea unlikely. The doors opened and the two women stepped out, Helen Gowers leading the way along the corridor to a large oak-panelled door. As she knocked, Cathy heard Dan's low, slightly impatient 'Come in,' with a leaping of all her senses. Helen Gowers stood back, smiling blandly at Cathy, waiting for her to step into the room. It was too late to back out now, so taking a deep, shaky breath, Cathy entered the room and shut the door behind her.

Dan was standing at the window, his back turned to her, and she remembered with a twisting of her heart that he had been in exactly that same position at their final confrontation in Los Angeles. She stared at the power and the strength of his body beneath the dark expensive suit he wore, at his proud dark head, and her own racing heartbeats deafened her, so loud that he must surely hear them. She was caught in the grip of a fierce, tearing emotion as she stared and stared. Her love had become even deeper, stronger in the eighteen months of their separation. It was a shock to realise that.

Dan was silent, but she sensed his awareness of her in the room. He was waiting for her to speak first.

'Hello, Dan.' Her voice was shaking, barely above a whisper, and she walked further into the room, nearer to him.

He turned then, a smooth slow movement, looking at her for the first time. 'Hello, Catherine,' he replied coolly, his voice impersonal, giving absolutely nothing away.

She looked into his dark face. He had not changed, his face was still incredibly attractive, lean and hard-boned, strongly defined, his mouth firm and sensual, perhaps a little cynical now, his hooded green eyes as enigmatic as always.

To look at him after all this time was devastating and she ached with love for him, ached to go into his arms and beg him to love her in return. She also knew for certain that the small measure of peace she had fought for over the past year and a half had been shattered completely as soon as she stepped into this room. She would return to Brighton as raw and as desperate as she had been when she left Los Angeles. Eighteen months' struggle destroyed in a second or two. She did not think she could cope with that long haul again.

She noticed then that Dan was staring at her, taking in the pallor of her pointed face, the feverish brightness of her eyes, her gentle mouth, before skimming over her neat hair and businesslike clothes.

'Sit down.' He indicated a chair far too near to him, but she could not refuse. 'Would you like a drink?'

She wanted to scream at his politeness, but she knew that she could never crack that calm control. He did not even seem surprised to see her. I'm your wife, she wanted to shout at him. I love you. Instead she stretched her lips in the semblance of a smile and said quite coolly,

'A cup of coffee would be nice.'

He inclined his head and pressed a button on the complicated-looking machine in front of him. 'Helen, two coffees, please.'

Cathy listened to the cool, drawling voice with a rush of unexpected pleasure, keeping her head lowered, her hands linked loosely on her lap. Only seconds later a light tap on the door heralded the arrival of Helen Gowers carrying a tray which she placed on the desk between them. 'Will that be all?' Her voice was soft, her smile brilliant, and Cathy felt angry, jealous as Dan smiled disarmingly back at his secretary.

'Yes, thank you, Helen.' The cool blonde left the room, obviously disappointed, her blue eyes hardening on Cathy as she turned from Dan.

Cathy watched him as he poured out coffee for them both, her eyes on his strong brown hands, curled round the fragile china cups. She did not know how to begin to ask him for money, she felt sure that she could not go through with it—it had been a crazy idea. Their hands touched briefly as he passed her the coffee and she nearly spilled it, as his touch, so impersonal, so accidental, seared through her like fire. It made her angry with him and with herself and, strangely, gave her courage. He can only say no, she told herself sternly. But as the silence stretched between them, that courage faded as quickly as it had come. Dan seemed to have absolutely nothing to say to her, his green eyes watchful, totally unreadable, the powerful line of his shoulders oddly tense beneath dark cloth.

'How ... how are you?' she asked suddenly, unable to bear his silence, his observation of her.

The firm mouth twisted. 'How polite you are, Catherine,' he observed mockingly. 'I'm sure it isn't of the slightest interest to you, but I'm fine. And you?'

She flushed, hurt by his mockery, wondering whether or not to defend herself and deciding against it. He could crush her so easily, she was too vulnerable to leave herself open to that sort of attack.

'I'm well, thank you,' she replied in a small, stilted voice.

Dan observed the slow flush of colour in her cheeks with detached eyes, offering her a cigarette which she refused and lighting one for himself with a smooth graceful movement. 'Yes, you look well, just as beautiful as I remember,' he remarked expressionlessly, as though making it clear that her beauty could not affect him in any way at all. Had it ever? she wondered dully, but remained silent. She felt so alone, so hurt and miserable to realise that they could not even talk to each other.

'Now that we've dealt with the pleasantries, perhaps you should tell me why you've come here,' he said, glancing at his watch. 'I have another appointment at three.'

'I'll be as brief as I can, then,' she retorted, stung into bitterness.

Dan's eyebrows lifted. 'Good.' He was calm, quiet, uncaring.

'You're not going to give me any help are you?' she cried, on the verge of tears.

'Why should I? You walked out on me, re-member?'

Cathy bit her lip savagely, tasting her own blood. Dan had twisted the facts of their wrecked mar-riage to benefit himself. She could not believe how cold and heartless he was. 'Dan . . . I. . . .'

'Tell me what you want, Cathy, and then go.' His voice was suddenly harsh, rough with an emotion she could not recognise or define.

'I need some money,' she blurted, wanting only to get this painful disastrous meeting over with.

His eyes sharpened on her vulnerable face. 'How much?'

'Twenty-three thousand pounds,' she whispered, her eyes fixing on his lean face with bruised inten-sity.

He did not seem shocked or surprised, but threw back his coffee in two mouthfuls before replying. He might have been made of stone for all the emo-tion he betrayed.

'Why do you need so much money?' he asked calmly.

'Will you lend it to me?' Her voice was desper-ate—she had to know.

'Tell me why you need it,' he repeated im-placably, staring at her.

He was calling the tune and she had no choice but to obey him. She wondered if she could make up a story, but found that she couldn't lie to him. Eighteen months ago she had been the best liar in the world. It was almost funny.

'Joe . . . Joe is in trouble, he's been gambling heavily and he's now in debt for twenty-three thousand pounds. I'm afraid for his safety, he seems to think that if he doesn't pay. . . .' Her voice trailed off, her mind refusing to conjure up the images that had been haunting her.

'So he runs to you with his tail between his legs.'
Dan was sardonic. 'Why didn't he come here himself?'

'He thought there was more chance of you lend-
ing the money to me,' she replied truthfully, caught
off balance and cursing her honesty as the words
left her mouth.

Dan smiled, a cynical twisting of his lips. 'Why
should he think that?'

Cathy flushed, unbearably embarrassed. 'Is the
answer no, then?' Her eyes were filled with tears
and she could not see him properly. He did not
answer, so she assumed that it was. She stumbled
to her feet, making her way blindly towards the
door, but his hand closed roughly on her arm
before she had taken two steps, hauling her round
to face him, hurting her, yet filling her with an
aching longing, his touch searing through the fab-
rics that covered her skin.

Her nerves, her emotions, her shaky control all
seemed to snap at his touch and her tears fell unchecked, soaking her pale face in an unexpected
rush. Dan swore violently.

'Tears, Catherine?' he enquired bitterly. 'Not
worthy of you.' The words cut into her, hurting
her terribly, making her cry even more, unable to
stop herself now, her hands lifting in a small convulsive gesture of sad defeat.

She heard Dan sigh, wanting to get away from
him, but unable to push his hand from her arm.
The next moment she was in his arms, her dark
head pressed to his wide shoulder. He held her
tightly, with a kind of fierce necessity, his arms
heavy bands of steel, his hard body familiar and
comforting and very disturbing.

She let herself forget the anger and the bitterness between them. She had waited for ever, it seemed, to know his comfort, his strength again, and her tears fell faster as everything seemed to explode inside her, millions of tiny pieces that would not fit together any more.

In the end there were no more tears left, she was dry and miserable with no excuse to remain in his arms. She lifted her hand and pushed at his hard chest, feeling regret as the hand that had been stroking so gently over her hair dropped and he released her. She immediately regretted her move, feeling totally bereft as he moved back behind the desk.

'I'm so sorry,' she sniffed awkwardly, pulling a tissue out of her handbag and wiping her face.

'Forget it.' The harsh note was still in his voice, but he sounded sincere.

She bit her lip. 'I'd better go . . . it's nearly three . . . I. . . .'

'Sit down and shut up,' Dan interrupted mildly. Cathy did not think, but obeyed, watching him through wary, red-rimmed eyes, sure that she looked a positive sight. A humiliating thought.

'If I give you the money. . . .' he began, and her heart lifted.

'I don't want you to give it to me, I want a loan,' she said gravely, her eyes wide and hopeful.

'How do you propose to pay it back?' Dan queried softly.

'I could pay so much a month.' She sighed, realising the enormity of such a thing. 'It would take some years, but I'd do it, I wouldn't let you down, I promise.' She was touching in her eagerness and Dan stared at her, unable to drag his eyes away.

'No, that won't do, it's totally unrealistic,' he said harshly.

'But why? I can't pay you back any other way.' Had he built up her hopes merely for the pleasure of dashing them.

His hard face was implacable. 'There's only one way I'll give you the money, either you accept it or there's no deal. Understand?' The eyes that held hers were without expression, the brilliant green depths totally blank.

'What is it?' she asked, feeling uneasy now. She might have known there would be strings attached.

'Your brother will work for me—a publicity job, based in L.A. He'll start immediately and it will be up to him to pay back the loan, not you—is that clear? It's a good job, well paid, it shouldn't be too much of a wrench—he's not the world's best photographic journalist from what I hear.' Dan's voice was clipped, faintly amused, and Cathy frowned, wondering at his motives. At least if Joe worked for Dan, Dan would be sure of getting his money back. Los Angeles was a long way away, though; she would hardly ever see her brother. Who would look after him, who would he turn to when he was in trouble?

'I don't know. . . .' she began, her eyes shadowed with worry.

'Cathy, you have to let go. He's not a kid any more, he's an adult. You won't always be there and the sooner he learns that the better. I'll keep an eye on him for you,' Dan said gently.

She knew the truth of what he was saying, but she was in no mood to hear him rubbing it in. 'Oh, I see, this is a purely selfless suggestion, your only motives being to help my brother,' she flashed sarcastically.

'On the contrary,' Dan actually smiled, 'that's only part of the deal.'

'What more do you want—blood?' she flung at him. He had her over a barrel and she was angry and worried. Why couldn't he just agree to a straight loan? He was going to make her suffer for spoiling his plans and walking out on him.

'I want you to come back and live with me as my wife.' He saw her stricken expression, the question in her eyes. 'Oh, don't worry, I don't want your body,' he said cruelly. 'But I do need a hostess for business purposes. I have very lucrative contracts in the Middle East—it's well known that I'm married, and separation and divorce are not recognised there. I can't afford to have my reputation as a reliable businessman tarnished by the fact that my marriage is finished. You will live with me as the other condition of the loan.'

It was a bombshell, the last thing she could have imagined, and for a moment she could not take it in. To live with Dan again. . . . She couldn't do it!

'Why can't Natalie be your hostess?' she asked tiredly, still confused, but realising that he was echoing what Natalie had told her that morning in Los Angeles. A man in Dan's position needed a wife. Truthful, bitchy Natalie, she thought icily.

'Natalie is not my wife,' Dan replied levelly.

'Is that why . . . is that why you've never asked for a divorce?' she queried painfully, as the thought suddenly struck her, remembering her fear that one day he would.

'Of course,' he replied smoothly. 'Did you think otherwise?'

'No,' she said quickly, too quickly.

His green eyes sharpened on her face. 'Surely you didn't expect me to make it easy for you and your lover by filing for divorce? Tell me, Cathy, doesn't he object to you wearing my wedding ring?'

She coloured brightly, stung by his open mockery, and hid her hand immediately. Sometimes it was hard to remember that he believed all her lies about herself. He believed that she loved somebody else—it was incredible! His image of her life was fictional, a fairy story created by her, a terrible mess. 'I don't want to talk about it,' she got out stiffly.

Dan's mouth tightened, as he misunderstood her, fury stiffening his body. 'Hard luck, sweetheart, you're going to have to. Your lover will have to go—as far as the world is concerned, you and I will be happily married.'

'I haven't agreed to do it,' Cathy said desperately, her heart racing, as everything gradually sank in. He was moving too fast for her.

'But you will—after all, what's the alternative? Joe won't get off lightly if he doesn't pay his debts,' said Dan, his eyes relentless.

'Stop it, I don't want to hear!' she cried, pressing a hand to her cold forehead.

He shrugged indolently, uncaringly. 'That's the deal, Catherine, take it or leave it. Your brother will work for me and you will live with me as my wife. Both of you will sign certain documents before I pay off the casino.'

'For how long would I have to . . . to live with you?'

'Until the loan is repaid,' he said coldly, inflexibly.

It would take years and she could not bear it. If she went back to live with him she would be in exactly the same position as she had been in before she left him. She still loved him desperately, he still did not care for her, still loved Natalie. It was impossible, totally impossible. But what choice did she have?

'I couldn't bear it,' she whispered half to herself.

'It's up to you.' His mouth compressed tightly as she insulted him.

'Dan, please, there must be some other way. . . .'

'There's no other way, Catherine—dammit, will it really be so hard for you? I will make no demands on you except that you be there when I need you. You will be wealthy, well cared for, I'm offering you a very easy life, a small price to pay for your brother's safety.' He was angry, his body taut, his green eyes shadowed, flashing. From his point of view, her life with him would be easy, but if only he knew!

'I'll have to talk to Joe about it,' she said defeatedly, stalling for time.

'I'm sure he'll agree,' Dan said drily, his anger draining away. He was too damned perceptive, Cathy thought, knowing that Joe would agree. No doubt he would see her position the same way Dan did and it would let him off the hook, his prime concern. Yes, he'd agree.

'You're too emotional,' Dan remarked coolly. 'This is a business deal, beneficial to us both, and the sooner you learn to look at it objectively, the easier it will be for you.'

It would never be easy. Cathy got to her feet, very tired and aware that her life, all her time, was out of her control again.

Dan stood up too, walking round the massive desk to stand in front of her, watching her through narrowed eyes. 'I'll contact you in a day or two and you can let me know your decision,' he said quietly, very businesslike.

She looked up into his face, dry-mouthéd at the hard, masculine beauty of him. 'Yes,' she said on a small sigh, searching his eyes for the triumph she had expected and, finding none, she felt surprised.

'I'll arrange for a car to drive you home,' Dan said gently.

'I can get the train,' she protested, dazed by his nearness, his potent sexuality.

'Don't argue, Cathy,' he smiled, taking her breath away. She gave in. There was no point in arguing with him. 'You haven't changed,' he said oddly, his voice soft, still staring down at her.

'That's not what my friends say.'

'Perhaps they don't know you as well as I do,' he taunted, without malice, touching her cheek.

Cathy turned away in embarrassment, her pulses leaping at his careless touch. She did not answer him.

'I'm sorry, I didn't mean to embarrass you.'

Her head jerked round at his apology her eyes wide, widening further as he bent and touched his mouth gently to her forehead.

Ten minutes later as she leaned back against the soft leather upholstery in the back of the car he had arranged for her, she closed her eyes and thought about that kiss, her fingers moving automatically to her forehead. Why had he kissed her? She could not think of one good reason why he should, and it had dissolved her anger with him so completely.

The car picked up speed on the open road and she was glad that she had accepted his offer of transport home; she was really in no mood to do battle on the trains, not this afternoon. She wondered how she had taken his blackmail so calmly, but knew that she hadn't, her hand flying to her mouth to smother her instinctive cry, as the full implications sank in. She would be *living* with Dan, seeing him every single day, not free until Joe had repaid a vast sum of money—in other words, years and years.

She could imagine what it would be like all too vividly. It was a step backwards, and she hated Dan and Joe for forcing her, using her, manipulating her into this impossible position. She thought of herself at eighteen—was it really less than two years ago?—marrying Dan so innocently, pushing aside her serious self-doubts, only to have her marriage shattered within a couple of weeks. She had wanted to forget, but there was no chance of that now.

She lit a cigarette, despising her own self-pity, and tried to think positively. She loved Dan, even though she knew him to be a ruthless, heartless swine. Perhaps, and her mind seized on this desperately, perhaps if she lived with him again she would be able to root out her love, killing it and freeing herself for ever. She knew what kind of a man he was now, there could be no disillusionment, so she would use her enforced time with him as ruthlessly as he would, to free herself of the love that had ruined her life. It was the best she could do.

She saw Joe the next day. He came to her house, in the evening after work. Cathy had hardly slept at all the previous night and had spent the day trudging along the beach, thinking and thinking and trying to sort things out, until she felt that she was going insane. Consequently her temper was rather short and she had to quell her feelings of irritated resentment when she opened the front door and saw him smiling hopefully at her.

'Come in.' She could not manage a smile but walked into the sitting room, leaving him to close the front door and follow.

'Shall I make some coffee?' he asked cheerfully, as they stood together in the small room.

'If you like.' Cathy did not care.

'Sit down and relax, you look tired. Would you like something to eat? A sandwich?' He was trying to get round her, it was almost pathetic.

'No, nothing to eat.' She sat down as instructed and lit a cigarette. She had not even been able to look at food all day.

'I won't be a second.' Joe disappeared into the kitchen and she heard him whistling as he made the coffee. She absently traced a square on the knee of her jeans, wondering how he would take the news that he had to move to America. He returned within five minutes, carrying two cups of instant coffee, then shrugged out of his coat, pushing his long hair out of his face as he sat down opposite to her.

'You saw him, then?' He looked at her expectantly.

'Yesterday.' She wasn't stalling deliberately, but she was finding it hard to begin.

'What did he say?' Joe sipped his coffee and she realised that he was nervous.

'He'll pay the debt on two conditions,' Cathy began cautiously.

'Great! I knew he'd do it for you. God, it's a weight off my mind, I can tell you.' Joe was ecstatic, his whole body sagging with relief. 'Thanks, Cath, I owe you one.'

'You haven't heard the conditions yet,' she said drily.

Joe smiled. 'I'll do anything to get those vultures off my back.'

Cathy felt a flash of anger. It wasn't only him; she would lose much more to get him out of trouble. He might well be prepared to do anything, but why should she have to do the same?

'Go on, tell me the worst,' he prompted.

Cathy sighed. 'You will have to work for Dan while you're repaying the loan. You'll have some sort of publicity job based in Los Angeles, starting almost immediately.'

'Good God!' Joe was stunned, and she stared at him, trying to gauge his reactions. He thought about it for a moment, then smiled crookedly, his shoulders lifting. 'Doesn't sound too bad, does it? I've been thinking lately that the paper's a bit of a dead end. Working in the States—wow, it could be the start of something big!'

Cathy stared at him in astonishment. 'You wouldn't mind?' she gasped.

Joe shook his head. 'It's a bit of a shock, I grant you, but the more I think about it the more I realise what a terrific opportunity it is—I could get to the top in an organisation like that. Good old Dan!' He was miles away, talking himself into it by the second, hardly able to believe his luck, it seemed.

Cathy frowned, torn between relief that he hadn't taken it badly and anger that he actually *wanted* to go.

'There is another condition,' she reminded him stiffly.

Joe raised his eyebrows, concentrating his attention on her with difficulty. 'Which is?'

'I . . . well, I. . . . He wants me to . . . to go back and live with him as . . . as his wife.' She faltered briefly, knowing a stab of pain at the way Dan had made it clear that he had no interest in her body.

'*What?*' This last piece of news shocked even Joe.

'One of the conditions of the loan,' Cathy said bitterly, praying with some illogical part of her brain that Joe would say it was too high a price to pay, that Dan could keep his loan. He didn't of course, he couldn't, it was his only way out.

'He must want you very badly,' was all he said, still in that same shocked voice. Cathy felt like laughing hysterically. What a joke! Dan felt nothing for her, absolutely nothing. He certainly did not want her, she was merely a useful pawn.

'How do you feel about it?' Joe asked uncomfortably.

'I don't want to live with him!' she retorted angrily, feeling lost at the very thought of it. 'How do you think I feel about it?'

'You still love him,' Joe reminded her. 'It may be an opportunity to put things right between you.'

'And that would suit you fine, wouldn't it? You get your gambling debts paid off, a cushy job in L.A. and the satisfaction of knowing that you've brought Dan and me together again. Very neat and very smug,' she flashed, losing control of her temper.

Joe moved restlessly, his face flushed, not looking at her. 'I didn't mean. . . .' he began.

'No, you never do. You don't seem to realise that everything I've built up over the past eighteen months is destroyed, and all because you were trying to impress some redhaired model!' She regretted it as soon as she said it. She had spoken in anger, not calculating cruelty, and she had hurt him, reminding him of a woman he had loved, and was trying to forget.

'I'm sorry, Cath,' he mumbled, obviously very uncomfortable.

'I'm sorry too. What I just said—well, it was uncalled for. I don't know what to do, you see, I'm at my wits' end.' She was appealing for his help.

Joe got to his feet. 'I'd better be going.' He did not want reminding of what she was going to do for him. He could not help her at all.

'Yes, of course. Contact Dan about the job as soon as possible,' she reminded him dully, wishing that he would stay and talk it over with her.

'I will.' He lowered his head, avoiding her eyes. 'And thanks. I'll try and make it up to you some day. If there was any other way. . . .' Then he was gone, and Cathy knew with miserable certainty that she had damaged their relationship beyond repair with her anger, however well justified it had been. Everything seemed to be going wrong, she thought as she began to cry. Everything.

The next morning she telephoned Greg and invited him over for dinner that evening. She had to explain to him that she would be going back to live with Dan—she owed him that for his quiet supportive friendship over the past months. She had decided to do it at a quiet, private dinner at her cottage; it was the best place for such a difficult explanation. Greg was pleased by her invitation and her heart sank a little. He would be there at eight o'clock sharp and he would bring the wine, he told her, and she could almost see the smile on his face as she rang off.

She dressed carefully that evening once the meal was prepared and in the oven, choosing a cream-coloured silk suit patterned with pale brown flowers and cream high-heeled sandals. She looped up her hair with tired hands, pinning it into a neat bun, knowing that Greg would be upset when she told him her news. It was going to be very difficult to pretend that it was her own decision, that she and Dan were happily reconciled. Almost beyond her capabilities, in fact.

Greg was on time, and stepped in from the cold night, his eyes skimming appreciatively over her slender, silk clad figure. He kissed her cheek, handing her the wine, and was so glad to see her that she felt like crying. Another payment to Dan— the loss of Greg's friendship. They sat by the fire, sipping sherry, and he told her about his work of the moment, asking about hers, light uninvolved conversation.

The meal, though not particularly special, was perfectly cooked, delicious, thick, home-made soup, steak with vegetables, cheese and fresh fruit. Greg enjoyed it, and ate heartily, not noticing that Cathy could barely manage more than a few choking mouthfuls. He insisted on helping her with the washing up and later they sat by the fire again, relaxed, replete, drinking coffee and brandy, and Cathy knew that the time had come for her news. She could not put it off indefinitely.

Greg was surprised and rather hurt, she could tell, but there was nothing he could do as she painted a rosy picture of her future with the husband she loved.

He was silent when he finished, and Cathy felt terrible. Although he had never revealed his feelings for her and she had never encouraged him to, she knew that he cared for her very much—too much.

The doorbell rang as she was apologising, the only thing she could think of to do, and she went to open it, relieved at the interruption, but frozen to the spot for a moment as she saw Dan outside.

'Hello, Catherine. Are we going to stand like this all night or are you going to let me in?' he smiled at her, his voice teasing. Her heart was beating very fast as she gazed into his lean face, incredibly surprised to see him. She held open the door, moving without thought, and he stepped inside, their bodies almost touching in the narrow hallway. He was wearing a dark grey suit and a dark tailored overcoat and he looked tired, she thought, with a rush of concern.

'What do you want?' she asked, not unkindly, unable to take her eyes off him.

'A drink would be appreciated,' he muttered, raking a hand through the gleaming darkness of his hair.

Cathy gave a defeated little sigh. 'I have a friend here,' she explained, turning away to lead him into the sitting room.

Dan's eyes narrowed on her face, catching her flush of embarrassment before she turned away. She regretted this meeting of Dan and Greg, it would hurt Greg. After what she had told him, he might even think that Dan's presence was deliberate.

Greg stood up as they entered the room, surprise on his face as he saw Dan behind Cathy. The two men faced each other as Cathy introduced them, shocked by the violence she saw in Dan's eyes.

'Greg, my husband, Dan Foreman. Dan, Greg Calvert.' They did not shake hands, merely nodded at each other, and a strange tension built between them, filling the room. Cathy stared at Dan's clenched jaw, at the tension, the threat in his powerful body. Greg saw it too, and a dull red flush crept along his cheekbones as he retreated, moving uncomfortably. 'I'll go now,' he said to Cathy. Dan was silent, watching Greg with cold, hooded eyes, as he talked to her.

Flashing Dan a poisonous glance, she went to the door with Greg, sorry that their friendship had to end this way. 'I'm sorry,' she said inadequately, as he pulled on his coat. 'I had no idea he was coming here tonight.'

Greg smiled. 'Don't worry, I understand how he feels. Good luck, Cathy, and if you ever need me you know where I am. Don't hesitate.' He went as though to kiss her, then drew back embarrassed, remembering. She knew in that instant that he was more than halfway to being in love with her, and her eyes filled with tears. Greg had been so kind, she hated him to go this way.

She reached up and pressed her mouth to his cheek in farewell. 'Goodbye, and thank you,' she whispered, choked with tears.

'Goodbye, Cathy.' He was gone quickly, disappearing into the night. She shut the door slowly, turning to find Dan leaning indolently against the door jamb, watching her as she swallowed back her tears.

'Very touching,' he remarked coldly, reinforcing her suspicion that he had been listening to her and Greg saying goodbye.

'How could you!' she burst out. 'You made him go, you made him feel so uncomfortable that he had to leave!' She was aching with sadness for hurting Greg; he had not deserved it. She turned tear-filled, accusing eyes on her husband. 'Why did you do it?'

Dan's face hardened. 'It was part of the deal. He had to go.' His voice changed then, becoming cold, taunting. 'You had him on a string, didn't you, Cathy, on his knees, wanting you.' She recoiled from the harshness in his voice, shocked by what he said. Dan had noticed within seconds of meeting Greg what it had taken her months to realise.

'You're so damned clever, aren't you?' she taunted bitterly, moving past him into the warm sitting room, shivering from head to foot. Dan followed, his movements smooth and furious.

'If you wanted a fool you should have married him, not me,' he drawled hurtfully.

Cathy turned on him. 'You swine!' she spluttered. 'I certainly don't want you!'

It was a mistake to goad him, she knew that. Too late. His body stiffened, the green eyes holding hers, suddenly darkening with anger as he reached for her, roughly, convulsively, one hand tangling in her hair, pulling back her head, uncaring that he hurt her as his mouth moved savagely over hers, parting her lips with merciless expertise, grinding the inner softness of her mouth against his until she could taste her own blood. She heard him groan, a low hoarse sound in his throat as he too tasted the rusty tang of her blood, then his mouth gentled against hers, becoming warm and persuasive, disturbingly sensual.

Cathy could not help but respond, her small hands moving without volition to frame his lean face, her mouth moving softly beneath his, as a familiar aching warmth flooded her body.

'Tell me now that you don't want me,' Dan murmured against her mouth, his breath warm and clean and somehow erotic against her face.

Cathy stiffened, aware that she had been tricked, and pulled away from him in anguish and silence.

He let her go easily. 'I hate you!' she whispered with passionate intensity.

The room was very silent; she could hear Dan breathing, a rough uneven sound. 'That's unfortunate.' His voice was cool, unfathomable. 'Because I've come for your decision. I have to know tonight.'

CHAPTER EIGHT

THREE days later Cathy moved back into Dan's penthouse apartment in London. Joe had flown out to Los Angeles the day before, and Cathy had to admit that Dan moved fast. Arrangements had been made with lightning speed, she had barely time to breathe, and her only consolation was that Joe was now out of danger with the casino, the debt having been paid off in full by Dan, the morning after she had agreed to his conditions.

She had seen Joe off at the airport, terribly sad to see him go and strangely suspicious that Dan was trying to isolate her, smoothly getting rid of her friends, first Greg, now Joe, so that she only had him left to turn to. It hardened her resolve that he would never know how she felt about him and she would never, ever turn to him for comfort, advice or friendship. Never.

Joe was excited, almost boyish in his enthusiasm for his new life, and did not seem particularly miserable to say goodbye to her. He kissed her cheek, hugging her tightly, then he was gone, waving cheerfully, and she was left with the empty ache of tears in her throat. How could he be so carefree?

Dan was waiting for her in the car, cool and remote, and she averted her face, staring out of the window. 'It won't be long before you see him again,' he had reassured her. 'We'll be flying out ourselves next month.'

'Thanks for telling me,' she had muttered ungraciously, her voice tearful as she refused his comfort.

Now she stood in the luxurious empty flat, staring out of the window at the bustle below. Dan had left before she woke that morning, she had not even seen him, and that *should* have been a relief. The place had not changed much since she had last been here—her wedding night, she remembered with a twisting heart; a couple of new pieces of furniture, different paintings in some of the rooms, but apart from that it was exactly the same— beautiful, masculine, alien to her. Cathy turned away from the window and wandered through the place, room after room, touching things, looking at things, wondering if Dan ever did buy a house in England. Her hand faltered on the doorknob of his bedroom, the room where they had made love, and driven by something she didn't understand, she stepped inside.

The blinds were closed, the room dim, and she stared round, remembering everything with painful clarity. The huge bed was unmade, one pile of pillows in the centre bearing the indentation of Dan's head. She walked over to the bed and lay down exactly where he had lain the previous night. It was devastatingly intimate, and her mind filled with memories of his lovemaking, taunting her, weakening her until she turned her head into the pillows and cried her heart out, and it was a long time before she roused herself and left the room.

Later that morning she wrote to Holly. She had

been meaning to write for ages, but her time had been short. Holly had married Garth, Julia's brother, the object of her attention at the party where Cathy had met Dan. They lived in Canada now, though both girls were anxious not to lose touch. In her letter Cathy briefly explained that she and Dan were reconciled and living together again. *If I say it enough and write it enough,* she thought with a grimace, *I'll probably end up believing it myself!*

Dan came home late that evening, tired and tense. Cathy was in the bath when he arrived and re-entered the huge lounge to find him sitting in one of the soft leather armchairs, twirling a glass of Scotch in his hands, his eyes closed. She moved silently into the room on bare feet, her attention caught and held by the dark lashes that fanned his cheeks. She pulled the belt of her satin wrap tighter and turned to leave, but his eyes snapped open, as though he had sensed her presence, his dark gaze travelling slowly over her, taking in her long, loose wet hair, clean face, the satin wrap that did not hide the curved perfection of her body, and her long bare legs and feet. She flushed under that unnerving gaze, wanting to run and hide, but stopping herself short. She did not want him to know the effect he had on her; he had forced her to live with him, so why should she keep out of his way? She would treat the place as if it was her home. She strolled over to the table and poured herself a small measure of Scotch and a very large measure of ginger ale, part of her reckless mood, then curled herself up on one of the chairs and smiled at him, brilliantly.

'How was your day?' She congratulated herself on her calmness. She could really get quite good at acting, it might even lead to a career in films, she thought hysterically.

Dan stared at her. 'Successful,' he drawled softly. 'And yours?'

'Fairly boring,' she replied in a bright, empty voice, sipping her drink and watching him over the rim of the glass.

'Raoul called. Joe started work this afternoon, he seems to be settling in okay,' Dan told her.

Cathy's face softened. 'Good. Could I telephone him tonight?'

'Yes, you can call him whenever you like, you don't have to ask,' he said gently.

'How is Raoul?' She did not want his gentleness, it destroyed her, so she changed the subject.

'Working hard for me,' came the amused reply.

Dan knew what she was up to, she thought angrily, and he was playing her along. Well, two could play at that game, she would soon knock that smug smile from his face.

'Tell me how Natalie is,' she said sweetly.

Dan smiled. 'You never liked her, did you?'

'What makes you say that?' she parried, sure that she had never revealed her dislike to him. Maybe Natalie herself had told him.

'Come on, Cathy.' Dan suddenly sounded tired. 'We should be past the stage of playing games with each other.'

She frowned. 'Very well, you're right, I never have liked Natalie, she was never very kind to me.' She had the feeling that Dan had somehow turned the tables on her, that she was not in control of their conversation any more, which meant that if she was not careful she would find herself treading very dangerous ground.

'Kind?' He picked up on that word curiously. 'Explain.'

She moved restlessly on the couch, feeling embarrassed. 'I don't really want to talk about it,' she muttered, staring into her glass. What would he say if she hurled her accusations at him? No good could come of it, she would only reveal her love, her jealousy. He had made it clear that Natalie was not a subject he wished to discuss with her. It suited her fine, just fine.

'What would you like to talk about then?' Dan asked, his eyes careful, watching her, his voice faintly indulgent. 'Tell me how the rest of your family are,' she begged.

His face sobered. 'Owen died six months ago—I thought you knew.'

'Oh God, no, I didn't know. Dan, I'm so sorry.' She was shocked by the news and she felt very spiteful for being so rude about Natalie. 'What happened?'

'He seemed to be recovering from the heart attack he had before you left L.A. He'd only been home a couple of months after convalescence when he had another one, and he was dead before he reached hospital.'

Cathy watched the grief in his eyes, the darkness of pain. She had not known, how could she? Obeying her instincts, she moved to his side and shyly touched his hand, wanting to give him comfort. He took her hand in both of his, his fingers caressing her skin gently, touching the heavy band of gold on her wedding finger.

'We have to find some way out of this God-awful mess,' he muttered wearily. Cathy did not understand what he was talking about. She was dazed by his nearness, his fierce attraction, and lifted her free hand to touch the hard bones of his face, feeling them tighten under her fingertips, as she leaned forward and kissed his mouth. He stiffened, perfectly still, not touching her, not responding for a second.

Appalled, as she came to her senses by her own courage, her own wantonness, Cathy drew back, but Dan's arms suddenly came round her, his mouth finding hers in one fierce movement, his lips parting hers with desire and a terrible hunger.

There was no anger between them, and she clung to him blindly, responding, kissing him back passionately, until he released her and moved away abruptly, striding across the room to pour himself another drink. Cathy did not look at him, certain that he had rejected her. Instead, she got shakily to her feet and fled the room, feeling cold and lonely and miserable. Dan left the flat about half an hour later, and did not return until late. Cathy lay in bed, staring up at the ceiling, hearing him come in and go straight to his bedroom. It was impossible.

A week later Natalie and Larry arrived from America. Dan had told Cathy about their visit and although she was looking forward to seeing Larry again, her heart had sunk at the news that Natalie would be with him. 'Don't worry about me, I won't get in the way,' she had assured him tightly, knowing that if Natalie stayed in the flat, it would break her heart. 'What are you talking about?' he had queried frowningly. She had refused to answer, sure that he was being deliberately obtuse. Fortunately she later learned that both Natalie and Larry were staying with friends in London.

Larry came to visit her on the afternoon of his arrival. Dan was working and she opened the door with a happy smile, surprised at the rush of affection she felt for Dan's father. She made some coffee and on hearing that he had not eaten, insisted on cooking him a Spanish omelette. He seemed very glad to see her again and they chatted while he ate. It was a relief, for she had not been sure how he would take the news of their supposed reconciliation. She watched him fondly; he was so like Dan. He finished the omelette and leaned back replete. 'That was great,' he smiled. 'And how are you, Cathy—you look thinner, but just as lovely.'

She flushed at the compliment. 'I'm fine, and being slender is fashionable you know.' She paused, then said, 'I was so sorry to hear about Owen. I had no idea—Dan told me last week and I couldn't believe it.'

'We all miss him, especially Natalie. It hit her very hard, she's only just getting over it now,' Larry said slowly. Then he smiled, not wanting to depress her. 'I'm so glad you and Dan are back together again.'

Cathy smiled back at him. Presumably Dan had not mentioned the loan to his father. 'Thank you, I'm glad too,' she lied, wishing that she didn't have to, wishing she could be honest with him.

'Dan took it very badly when you left.' He saw her surprise. 'Oh, I know, he's strong, difficult to read, but it was clear to anybody with eyes in their head that he was suffering. But then you know how he loves you. He's always been a dreamer—I expect you know that as well.'

Cathy swallowed, close to tears. Larry had no idea about the affair Dan was having with Natalie. How beautiful it would be if she could believe what Larry said, if Dan did love her.

'I met your brother yesterday,' Larry went on. 'He seems like a fine young man. Raoul will look after him, you know, you mustn't worry.'

Cathy smiled. She had telephoned Joe a number of times since he left. He was enjoying himself thoroughly and she was becoming increasingly aware that she had no need to worry about him any more. The conversation was turned to safer topics and they chatted together all afternoon. While they talked there remained in the back of Cathy's mind the thought that Dan had suffered when she left him. She could not believe it, but it tantalised her as she tried to work it out.

Dan came in at six-thirty, offering to take them both out to dinner, and Cathy left the two men alone to talk while she took a shower and changed.

The evening was a great success. Larry's presence took away the tension between her and Dan and she could relax and enjoy both men's company. She found that she could not take her eyes off Dan; he filled her mind and her senses to the exclusion of all else. He looked tall and powerful in a black velvet evening jacket and dark trousers, and she felt the full force of his masculine sexuality. Coincidentally she also wore black, a figure-hugging cashmere dress with a thin gold belt, that she knew suited her to perfection.

As she listened to the men talking, sipping her wine and enjoying the delicious food, she was aware of Dan's eyes upon her, narrowed, unreadable, watching her almost all the time. It was unnerving, but it sparked off a deep sweet excitement inside her that became like a drug she needed as the hours sped by.

It was time to return home all too soon. They dropped Larry at his friend's house and drove back to the apartment in silence. Dan was quiet, seemingly preoccupied, his stark profile remote as she glanced at him covertly.

She lit a cigarette and relaxed against the soft leather upholstery, congratulating herself for handling this potentially disastrous situation so coolly. Her acting, so far, had been brilliant. Dan would never know how she cried her heart out nearly every night in the privacy of her own room.

As soon as they got back she escaped to bed almost immediately, murmuring goodnight at the broad length of his back and not waiting for an answer. But as she lay alone in her bed she ached for him so badly that her hands clenched by her sides, the nails digging painfully and unnoticed into the softness of her palms. Tonight she had let her careful guard slip, had let herself see Dan clearly for the fiercely attractive man that he was. Larry's easy company, the wine and the soothing surroundings had all contributed to the relaxing of the wall she had built around herself. It was so easy to think of him as a cold cruel monster, but tonight she had seen again his warmth, his charm, his gentleness, and it had left her devastated, weak with longing for him, uncaring for what he had done in the past.

Her body twisted restlessly between the smooth sheets. Damn, damn, damn! She would not sleep. Sighing, she slid out of bed and walked over to the window, pulling up the blinds and gazing out over London. It was late, but the city was still alive, bright, full of people.

Cathy rested her forehead against the cold glass. It was too hot, she would have to turn down the central heating. Living in her windy cottage by the sea, she had grown used to cold nights when the only warmth was inside the bed and one woke with a freezing cold nose. I'm just not used to luxurious living any more, she told herself wryly. Perhaps a hot drink would help, she pondered, knowing full well that it wouldn't help at all. Still, it would give her something to do, pass the time. She had the feeling that it was going to be a very long night. She opened her bedroom door quietly and peered out into the darkness. The apartment was totally silent and she assumed that Dan was in bed. She crept noiselessly into the large kitchen and switched on the light. Hot milk—that was supposed to help you sleep. She opened the huge refrigerator that was at least two feet taller than she was, and pulled out a bottle of milk. While it boiled, she let her eyes wander round the room. It was a dream of a kitchen, she had to admit—oak units, every imaginable kitchen device, plenty of space. Obviously designed by a woman, she thought, which somehow made her laugh. Her milk was starting to bubble and she pulled the pan off the heat. She did not hear the door swinging open, totally unaware of any other presence in the room until a low cool voice said, 'Any of that going begging?'

Cathy almost jumped out of her skin, she was so cocooned in her own thoughts. She spun round, a hand pressed nervously to the fluttering pulse in her throat.

'You . . . you frightened the life out of me!' she whispered breathlessly. He was wearing only a dark, silken robe, tied loosely at the waist, leaving bare most of his broad chest and powerful legs. The silk looked strangely fragile, sensual against his smooth brown skin, and her heart began to pound deeply, languorously.

'Sorry.' His brief hard smile told her he wasn't.

'Do you want some milk?' She turned back to

the hob, unaccountably flustered.

'Any chance of some coffee?' he asked persuasively.

'That won't help you sleep,' she told him sternly.

'Who said I wanted to sleep?' Dan drawled, his voice laced with laughter.

Cathy did not look round. 'I'll make some coffee,' she said, wishing that her voice didn't sound so breathless, so husky. It seemed to give her away. She switched on the percolator and tried to think where the cups were kept. Remembering, she turned round, to find Dan standing right in front of that particular cupboard. He was leaning back, his arms folded across his broad chest, watching her.

Cathy moved gracefully towards him, flushing brightly as she saw his eyes sliding appraisingly over her body. The thin lace of her nightdress was practically transparent in the bright light, she might as well have been naked, she thought hotly, wishing she had thought to put on her dressing gown.

As Dan's smokey green eyes returned to her face she saw that he was daring her to run from him, reading her mind as he had always been able to do.

She frowned at him. 'The central heating in this place is set far too high.'

He laughed, his beautifully-moulded mouth twisting with amusement. 'You can always turn it down,' he teased softly.

'I intend to,' she retorted. She was right in front of him now, her mouth dry as she stared up into his face. 'Cups—in the cupboard behind you,' she managed through dry lips. Dan smiled, twisting his body smoothly, and reached into the cupboard and handing her two mugs. 'Thanks.' She moved away from him as quickly as possible, her hands trembling as she made chocolate for herself and coffee for him.

Dan watched her in silence, not missing any of her jerky movements. She placed his coffee on the table, intending to drink her chocolate in her room. It was far too unnerving to stay in the kitchen with him. There was an unbearable intimacy in being alone with him, both of them only partly dressed, in a brightly-lit kitchen at two o'clock in the morning.

He touched her arm gently, blocking her exit. 'Stay and talk with me,' he said, not asking, not telling, but something very persuasive in between. All her instincts cried out against it, but she knew that it would be giving too much away not to stay as he requested.

'I'll get my dressing gown,' she said quietly.

Dan did not release her arm, his long fingers burning her skin. 'Cathy, you've already told me how hot it is in here, and that nightdress is perfectly respectable.' His cool green eyes reminded her of what he had said in his office. He did not want her body.

Shrugging defiantly, she sat down at the polished wooden table and sipped her chocolate, her fingernails nervously following the woodgrain. Dan sat opposite her and the silence and the tension seemed to grow as the seconds ticked by.

Cathy moved restlessly. 'We have nothing to talk about,' she said very quietly, not looking at him.

'No? I'd say we have a hell of a lot to talk about.'

'Like what?'

'Tell me about Greg Calvert. Was he the man you left me for?' Dan's voice was very soft, deadly.

This was dangerous ground indeed. She should have obeyed her instincts and got out when she could.

'Why do you want to know? I don't think it's any of your concern,' she answered stiffly, her mind working overtime, wondering what she would say if he persisted. He did.

'It is my concern, you're my wife.'

'Only because you forced me to come back to you,' she muttered, glaring at him.

Something flickered in his eyes. 'You married me of your own free will,' he reminded her coldly, a muscle jerking tightly in his jaw. 'And you still haven't told me about Calvert. What attracted you to him, apart from the fact that you had a chain round his neck? Is that where you like your men, Cathy, on their knees?'

The deliberately cruel, taunting words hit home, hurting her and reminding her of how shabbily she had treated Greg. 'Greg is kind, something you know nothing about. I miss him, he was a good friend, and despite what you think I had no idea how he felt about me until that last evening,' she said, her eyes filling with tears. Why was she justifying herself to Dan?

The dark brows lifted. 'You slept with him for over a year and didn't know how he felt about you?'

There was something in that cool mocking voice that snapped her temper and she chose her words unwisely. 'I never slept. . . .' She stopped abruptly, her hand flying to her mouth, aware that he had tricked her once again.

'You never slept with him,' Dan finished for her, his voice rough with satisfaction.

Cathy hated him at that moment. 'No, I never

slept with him,' she conceded dully, knowing defeat. It was incredible that he thought she had. There would never be anybody else. How could he not know that? She suddenly felt very tired of all her deceit, of all the lies between them. She wanted him to know the truth even though it would serve no useful purpose. 'Dan, when I . . . when I came to you and asked you to let me go, I told you there was someone else. I was lying, there was nobody else,' she admitted quietly.

'I know,' Dan replied, just as quietly.

'You—you *know*?' She was astounded. 'But how?'

He raked a hand through his hair, intensely weary. 'I didn't know at the time, you really had me fooled with that letter,' he smiled bitterly. 'But when you got back to London I hired someone to watch you—I'm not proud of it, Cathy, but I had to know. You were not seeing anybody, and one look at you and Calvert together told me what I needed to know.'

It was a nightmare. He had known all along that she had been lying. He had stood back and let her make an utter fool of herself. It was too humiliating.

'How dare you,' she whispered, hot colour staining her pale cheeks. 'How dare you have me followed by some sordid, private detective! It's despicable, utterly despicable!'

'Cathy. . . .' He reached out and touched her arm, but she pushed his hand away, violently, 'Don't touch me!' she hissed at him, jumping to her feet and running to the door. Dan caught her easily in the darkness of the lounge, his hands cruel as he pulled her round to face him. Cathy kicked out at him with her bare feet, blind with anger and pain, struggling in the fierce grip of his hands, using the full weight of her body to get away from him. She caught him off balance as she aimed her feet at him, flinging her body against him. Still holding her, he could not regain his balance, and they both fell, seemingly in slow motion, down on to the thick carpet, and Cathy landed on top of him, the hard strength of his body knocking the wind out of hers, as he stopped her hitting the floor. Dan moved swiftly, so that she lay in his arms, gasping for air.

'Are you hurt?' His breath was cool on her cheek.

'No, just winded—I'll be fine—in a minute,' she managed in short gasps.

He helped her to her feet, her hands curling in shock against the warm bare skin of his chest. She saw him smile as he lifted her effortlessly into his arms and she smiled back. It was crazy, funny, easing the anger, dissolving the tension.

He carried her to her bed, where he laid her down gently, arching over her. 'Cathy, I'm sorry, God knows I'm not proud of what I did, but I was desperate. I couldn't let you walk away from me like that. You were too young, too innocent, I was afraid for you and I had to know the truth,' he said harshly.

'Why did you tell me?' She stared up at him, wide-eyed, touched by his concern.

'You told me the truth tonight, so you deserved truth in return—something new for us, I guess,' he smiled.

'I'm sorry too. I overreacted,' she said softly.

He searched her face for long moments, then bent over and kissed her forehead, his mouth gentle, warm. 'Thanks for being so kind to Larry,

I appreciate it.' Then he was gone, before she had time to answer.

Cathy lay on the bed exactly where he had put her and thought about it all. She had regretted her lies almost as soon as they had left her mouth. She had intended telling him the truth tonight—well, half the truth. He had already known it. It did not matter. He had been concerned enough to keep an eye on her when she left him, afraid for her on her own. That did not matter either, it showed that he cared in a strange way.

She had been angry because she thought Dan had made a fool of her. She had been wrong, it had never been his intention to humiliate her, it was not his way. He cared deeply for people, never deliberately hurting anybody. He need not have told her about the detective and she would never have known. It did not fit together. The only thing she did know for sure was that he did not love her. Nothing would ever change that.

CHAPTER NINE

At the end of that week, Dan announced one morning that they would be spending the weekend with one of his business associates.

They were eating breakfast together for the first time since Cathy moved in. She had expected some embarrassment, some stiffness between them after she had revealed that there had been nobody else and he had revealed that he already knew, but she had been mistaken.

Since that night Dan had been kinder, and their

life together had improved. They were polite strangers, easily keeping their distance from each other, never coming into close contact. They did not spend very much time together, a conscious effort by Dan, it seemed. He worked during the day and at night they usually went out together, but always with other people, friends, business colleagues. On these occasions, Dan was the perfect husband and as he took her arm, gave her his full, stunning attention, looked after her, she could almost believe that he loved her. It was a fantasy that was becoming far too important to her. He was very convincing, and she hated him for it, her heart always wincing in pain when they returned to the apartment and the act was dropped, Dan once again becoming the cool, remote stranger who did not care for her at all.

There was a kind of waiting stillness surrounding their lives as though both knew they were treading through a minefield. Sooner or later there would be an explosion. Cathy knew that she would be the casualty of that explosion and her nerves were constantly on edge. She was still working, but only part-time now, finishing the comissions she had undertaken, but not accepting any new ones. She was in no mood to work, especially to create, which took calmness and peace and time, none of which she had. She was not interested in work anyway, her relationship and whole situation with Dan was more important. She wanted to devote all her energy to sorting it out. Then she would be free to work as much or as little as she liked. Something had to give soon, they both knew it.

In consequence, she was surprised by this weekend trip, jerking her thoughts back to her breakfast and what he was saying. 'Are they good friends of yours?' she asked curiously.

'I've known Dave for years, you'll like both him and Melissa, I'm sure.' He smiled at her, gently reassuring.

'How long will we be staying?'

'We'll go tomorrow, Saturday, and leave on Sunday. Will you mind a weekend away?'

'No, I'm quite looking forward to it,' she replied, surprised to find that it was true. 'Where do they live?'

'Deep in the country—Wiltshire. It will be good for you, you look pale.' His eyes flicked over her face, carefully, and she lowered her eyes, trying to concentrate on her coffee.

'Why have they invited us?' she asked, anything to steer the conversation off herself.

'So many questions!' Dan teased, recognising her ploy. 'Dave's company is in trouble, he's asked for my help and I'll do what I can. The invitation has been open for a long time, so it's a good opportunity to kill two birds with one stone,' he finished with a slight smile.

Cathy looked into his face, her heart constricting painfully with love for him. 'I'd like to be your friend,' she said softly, throwing caution to the wind in a reckless moment, and a desire to be honest with him.

He stiffened, staring into her eyes. 'I want more than that,' he said slowly, roughly.

'I don't understand,' she frowned, searching his green eyes for her answer.

His face closed, blank again. 'Forget it,' he advised with a smile, and the moment passed, even though it stayed in her mind all day.

Natalie and Larry came to dinner that evening. Cathy had not seen Natalie since she arrived in

London and she was most definitely not looking forward to their meeting. She prepared the meal herself, even though Dan had offered to get caterers in. She enjoyed cooking and she did not want to have the whole day free to brood about the coming evening. She decided on avocado mousse, beef casserole and cherry gateau, followed by cheese and fresh fruit, simple yet delicious.

She wondered as she bathed whether Dan and Natalie had seen much of each other since Natalie had arrived in London with Larry. Presumably, before Cathy had moved back with Dan, they had stayed here together whenever they were in England. Dan at least had some tact. He could have brought Natalie here, but he hadn't. Where did they go to make love? A hotel? The very thought of him making love to Natalie turned Cathy's blood cold and she was sick with jealousy.

The worst part about it was that she had to be polite, even friendly to Natalie, for her own sake, for Larry's sake. It would call for her very best acting, the most brilliant performance of this whole fiasco.

She took a great deal of trouble with her appearance, careful make-up disguising the pale, sleepless circles beneath her eyes, a beautiful mask to hide behind, raven hair neat and shining and her favourite dress, scarlet silk and lace with long flowing sleeves and a flaring skirt that swirled around her long slim legs. It was a spectacular dress, desperately expensive, and it lent her a smouldering gypsy look which she enhanced with huge looped earrings in beaten gold. She looked good, ready for anything that Natalie could throw at her, she thought, pirouetting in front of the mirror before leaving her bedroom.

Dan was waiting for her in the lounge, wearing a dark, beautifully tailored suit. His eyes slid over her, narrowed, appreciative. 'You look beautiful,' he smiled, his tone purposely light. 'Natalie and Larry are on their way up. Can I get you a drink?'

'Sherry, please.' She could feel her stomach tightening.

He handed her a glass. 'Don't look so frightened, you'll be fine.'

Her startled eyes met his, searching for some clue to his reassurance, but there was none; the green eyes were warm but unreadable.

Then the room was full of people, it seemed. Natalie, tall and very beautiful in sapphire blue chiffon, her jewellery sparkling in the soft light and Larry, smiling, tall and distinguished-looking in a pale grey suit.

'Hello, my dear. You'll be tired of seeing me here.' He kissed her cheek.

'Never!' Cathy replied emphatically, smiling at him as her eyes darted to Natalie, who was kissing Dan's mouth in greeting. Natalie still loved him. Cathy saw the fever in her eyes, dying swiftly as she turned to Cathy.

'It's good to see you again, darling,' she said with no particular enthusiasm, and her cheek touched Cathy's very briefly in the semblance of a kiss.

'Hello, Natalie.' Cathy managed a stiff smile, then moved back. She could not bear to be too near to Natalie, there was something cold and dangerous about her tonight, or maybe it was her imagination, the knowledge that Natalie and Dan were lovers. Dan was handing out drinks—the perfect host, Cathy thought spitefully. Natalie was talking to her and she forced herself to listen.

'We were all surprised, isn't that true, Larry?

You two were always *so* secretive,' she was complaining in a sweet, little-girl voice. Cathy smiled blankly, not knowing what to say. Presumably this little charade was all for Larry's benefit, everybody else in the room knew exactly what was going on.

'A man and his wife belong together,' Larry said firmly, smiling at Cathy, taking the pressure off her.

'I couldn't agree more.'

Dan's voice was just behind her and she froze with surprise as his arm slid around her shoulders. What was he up to? Her eyes slid to Natalie who had watched Dan's action with a sharp frown. Had they argued? Was Dan trying to make her jealous? Cathy sighed, sick of her own involvement in these destructive games. She excused herself on the pretext of checking the meal, shrugged free of Dan's disturbing grasp and made for the kitchen. It was a haven of peace and quiet, and she sat at the table and rested her head lightly on her hands, wondering how she would cope with a whole evening of Natalie.

'Catherine, are you all right?' Dan had followed her and she closed her eyes, wishing that he would leave her alone.

'Yes, I am,' she snapped shortly. 'No thanks to you!'

He moved silently into the room and sat on the edge of the table, one leg swinging idly, as he stared at her. 'Meaning?'

'Have you and Natalie had a row?' she asked recklessly.

He frowned slightly, and that annoyed her further. He thought he was so clever!

'No, Natalie and I never row,' he replied mildly.

'That must make for a beautiful relationship,'

she flung at him, her eyes flashing.

'Beautiful isn't the word I'd choose,' Dan smiled at her.

'Oh, and what word would you choose?' Cathy didn't know why she was doing this, she would only hurt herself, but somehow she could not stop.

'Has Natalie upset you?' His eyes sharpened on her small, pointed face. Changing the subject, Cathy thought sourly.

'Not yet, but we still have the whole evening ahead of us,' she retorted bitterly.

'Don't let her hurt you, Cathy. Natalie's tough, you're not. Ignore her.' His voice was curiously gentle and he touched her hair as he spoke.

'I've tried to like her, but I can't. We'll never be friends, you must see that,' she said honestly, moving her head slightly so that his hand dropped.

'It doesn't matter. Natalie has very few women friends, I don't know why, some women are just like that.'

She stared at him curiously. 'You don't mind?'

He laughed. 'Dear sweet Cathy, you and Natalie are poles apart. Why should I mind if you can't be friends?'

Poles apart. Yes, they were poles apart. Dan loved Natalie, he did not love her.

'Well, that's fine, as long as you don't expect. . . .' Her voice was sharp with pain.

'I expect nothing,' Dan cut in expressionlessly, moving suddenly, gracefully. 'I'll give you a hand with the food.' End of conversation, Cathy thought, piqued.

The meal, thank goodness, was a great success. Natalie was polite and amusing, not at all nasty, which surprised Cathy, although she did not believe in Natalie's sincerity enough to let her guard down. In spite of all Natalie's efforts, Dan refused to be monopolised by her, chatting to his father and Cathy, his eyes disturbing, caressing whenever they rested on his wife. Once again she felt herself falling under his spell, a spell that would disappear in a puff of smoke as soon as they were alone to-gether. He could captivate her so completely, with-out exerting any effort at all, drawing her to him until she forgot everything except her love, his fierce masculine beauty.

Her heart sank like a stone when Natalie offered to help with the clearing away and washing up. Cathy's eyes sought Dan's, willing him to help, but he was talking to Larry, both men engrossed in each other. Thank goodness for the dish-washer, she thought fervently, otherwise she could have been trapped in the kitchen with Natalie for ages and ages. So Natalie piled the dinner dishes on to a tray and Cathy filled the dishwasher.

'That's a charming little dress,' Natalie remarked, leaning gracefully against the table as she watched Cathy work. 'You're lucky, I can't wear red myself.'

'Thank you. It was made for me by a friend,' Cathy replied politely. Natalie seemed in no rush to leave the kitchen, even though there was nothing more she could do to help. Cathy felt suspicious and she stacked the dishes as quickly as she could, anxious to escape, instinctively aware that it was not wise to be alone with Natalie. Her stomach still lurched sickeningly whenever she remembered the last time they had been alone, the cleverly planned shopping trip, when Natalie had taken such pleasure in revealing that Cathy's marriage was nothing more than a joke, a cover-up. Dan was right, Natalie was tough, and Cathy was not strong enough to fight her.

'Lovely kitchen, isn't it?' Natalie commented, apparently conversationally, as she looked around her. 'Dan's not a bad designer, considering it's not his line.'

'Dan designed this kitchen?' Cathy was surprised. She had been sure it was a woman's work.

'The whole flat,' Natalie revealed. 'Didn't he tell you?' Cathy was silent. 'Such a dark horse,' Natalie laughed. 'You must be glad to be back here.'

'I am. Are you glad I'm back here?' Cathy asked coolly, tired of Natalie's clever mockery, her barbed remarks, the hints that Cathy did not understand. If Natalie had something to say to her, and she undoubtedly did or she would not be wasting her time in the kitchen, then Cathy wanted her to get it over with as soon as possible.

'What do you think? I want Dan, I've always wanted Dan——' Natalie stopped abruptly, her eyes glittering feverishly. 'But I think I've made myself clear on that point.' The laughing mask was firmly back in place, Natalie firmly in control of herself again. Cathy was surprised at that momentary slip. Natalie was a desperate woman and suddenly, for no good reason, Cathy felt sorry for her.

'Natalie . . .' she began, but Natalie cut across her, unexpectedly vicious as she saw Cathy's sympathy.

'Don't spread your poison about me, darling, I know what you're trying to do, but it won't work.'

'I don't know what you're talking about,' Cathy said, shocked and helpless and wondering if Natalie was insane, ill.

'Dan warned me off you tonight,' Natalie said through clenched teeth. 'But your lies won't keep him—he's mine, he'll always be mine!'

Cathy stared at her, wide-eyed with horror. Natalie's eyes were violent, febrile, frightening. 'Excuse me.' Cathy walked from the kitchen, her legs actually shaking. She could not stay there any longer. She felt sure, now, that Natalie was ill. The atmosphere in the kitchen had been deadly, terrifying. Perhaps the death of her father, a broken meaningless marriage, her love for Dan, all these things were too much for her to cope with.

Cathy walked into the lounge and uncaring what implications he placed on it, went and sat next to Dan on the leather sofa, where she slid her hand into his, comforted and reassured by his nearness, his strength. He did not look surprised, but merely smiled at her, a brief gentle smile, his long fingers stroking over her wrist as he talked to Larry.

Five minutes later Natalie came out of the kitchen and back into the lounge. Her desperation was gone. I could have imagined it all, Cathy thought, watching the other woman, poised and smiling as she sat down. Cathy moved nearer to Dan, feeling vaguely depressed and decidedly threatened.

Natalie and Larry left early. Larry was tired and although she felt guilty, Cathy was glad to see them go. It had been one hell of an evening, she thought wryly, feeling totally drained and quite exhausted. Dan had warned Natalie off her. She had no idea why he had done it, but it brought a warm glow to her heart.

'Time for bed.' Dan's voice was low and amused, and she forced open her incredibly heavy eyelids to find him standing over her.

'Yes.' Her voice was sleepy and she could not manage more than one word.

Dan pulled her to her feet. 'The meal was fantastic, thank you.'

'It's what I'm here for,' she said, yawning.

'Is it?' There was an odd note in his voice.

'Of course. I like Larry,' she added inconsequentially.

'He's very fond of you,' Dan told her gently.

'Natalie hates me.' She swayed towards him, dead on her feet, hardly aware of what she was saying. He reached out and steadied her, propelling her towards her bedroom.

'Go to bed, Cathy,' he repeated gently, and lowering his dark head, brushed her lips briefly with his mouth.

She woke from restless sleep, feeling dull and heavy-eyed the next morning, aware that something important had been said or done the night before, but infuriatingly she could not fit it together, it stayed just beyond reach of her conscious mind. She lay in bed, going over what had been said, looking for the breakthrough, but the pieces still would not fit. She heard the knock on her door, still deep in thought, her forehead creased with concentration, answering absently.

Dan strolled in with a cup in his hand. 'Coffee,' he said, handing it to her.

Cathy looked up at him with surprised eyes. 'Thanks.' Her pulses raced at the sight of him in old denim jeans and an open-necked blue shirt. He looked lean and strong and fiercely attractive.

'We'll be leaving in about an hour,' he told her with a smile, his green eyes flaring as he looked down at her.

Her hair was tousled, wild and soft, tumbling around her small face. Her nightdress was a pale green silk and one of the thin straps had slipped from her bare shoulder, exposing the soft white swelling of her breast. She saw the hunger in his eyes and flushed brightly, her whole body responding achingly to it, as she jerkily pulled the sheet up under her chin.

'An hour, you say,' she mumbled, not looking at him.

'An hour,' he repeated, his face openly amused, and left the room.

Cathy drank her coffee, then showered and dressed in black corduroy trousers and Fair-Isle sweater, tying back her hair in a ponytail and applying a light make-up. Then she packed her overnight case, hoping that she would like Melissa and Dave.

It was a cold clear morning and as they left the flat, she huddled thankfully into her sheepskin coat. As they left London the traffic was busy, but soon they were on an open road, picking up speed. Cathy felt tired, her restless nights finally catching up on her. The speed of the road flew by, hypnotising her, and without realising it, she leaned back in the warm comfort of the car and fell asleep.

She woke, not knowing how much later, to find her head pillowed against Dan's shoulder, as the car slid silently to a halt. She sat up abruptly and looked round. They were parked outside a large stone house, surrounded by trees, miles from anywhere.

'Are we here?' she asked, her eyes huge and still sleepy as she stared at Dan. His mouth was wry, indulgent.

'No, but I want to show you this house.'

She got out of the car, the cold air making her shiver, and pulled her coat around her warm relaxed body. The house was beautiful, deserted.

She allowed him to take her hand and lead her inside, through the arched wooden door into a large empty hall. There was no furniture, no carpets, but still the house had a warm, welcoming atmosphere.

Dan was silent as they walked through the deserted rooms, their footsteps echoing on the dusty polished floorboards. Tall windows, breathtaking open views, carved fireplaces and vast empty spaces, all remained in her mind. Cathy felt drawn to the house, strangely at peace, calm and knowledgeable as she looked round with Dan.

'It's beautiful,' she said quietly, when at last they stood in the hall again, having slowly explored every room together.

Dan lit two cigarettes, the flare of light from the match he used shadowing and illuminating the stark planes of his face.

'You like it?' He was still and serious.

'Yes, it's full of love and happy memories.' She laughed selfconsciously. 'I can't really explain what I mean.'

'I know what you mean. I felt it the first time I stepped inside.' He smiled.

'Why is it empty?' Cathy drew on her cigarette and stared up at the ornate ceiling.

'I haven't had time to fix it up and move in,' Dan said quietly, watching her.

'It's yours?' Her eyes jerked to his face and he nodded.

'You're very lucky,' she said wistful yet happy for him.

'I'd like you to do the interior.' It was almost an order, softened only by the warmth in his eyes.

'I . . . I couldn't,' she stammered, surprised but decisive.

'Why not?' he queried sardonically. 'I've seen your work and I like it. I'm hiring you if you prefer it that way.' He was angry, and she could not understand why.

She could make this house so beautiful, even as she had walked through it. The ideas had formed in her mind, quickly, easily, it hardly ever happened that way, only in special places—two places, her cottage and this house. But she could not put so much of herself into this house knowing that Dan would bring Natalie here when it was finished. As usual he was asking far too much.

'I don't prefer it any way. I'm sorry, but I'm not for hire,' she replied dully, and walked out of the house, knowing a deep sadness at leaving. She sat in the car waiting for him, her eyes filling with tears. He slid in beside her, moments later, his movements gracefully violent, furious, the tyres of the car screeching in protest as they swung back on to the road.

The silence that lasted until they arrived at Melissa and Dave's house was filled with anger, flashing between them like lightning. Cathy did not look at him once, but stared straight ahead, feeling cold and bitter that he should be so insensitive, yet knowing that it was not intentional, which did not help. He did not know what he had done, it was something to do with her, not him.

As Dan had promised, Cathy took to Melissa and Dave immediately. They were warm and friendly and welcoming, a relief after the cold hostility in the car. Their house was deep in the countryside, huge, modern and architect designed.

'I'm so glad to meet you,' Melissa smiled as she showed Cathy where she could freshen up. 'I've been dying to see what you're like. Dan was one of the most elusive bachelors for far too long!'

Cathy laughed, hiding her pain, throwing herself into her old pretence. 'That's why I thought I'd better do something about him,' she joked. She liked Melissa, who was small and slim and obviously pregnant, with a short cap of fair hair and an infectious smile. 'Have you known Dan long?' she asked Melissa casually, as she tidied her hair.

'He and Dave used to work together, but that was years ago. I met Dan when Dave produced him as best man at our wedding. When I saw him I wondered whether I'd made the right decision marrying Dave. Dan smiled and I went weak at the knees—I still do!' Melissa laughed, only half serious.

'I know what you mean,' Cathy replied lightly, her eyes sparkling, knowing in that instant that she had found a friend.

'I didn't forgive Dave for weeks for keeping Dan hidden until it was too late,' Melissa giggled. They joined the men soon after, and the day passed quickly and happily.

Dave was tall and athletic with light brown hair, a moustache and a dry wit that had Cathy and Melissa in peals of laughter every time he opened his mouth. They were madly in love and very, very happy, Cathy thought as she watched them together, her heart twisting with longing. We should be like that, she thought, staring at Dan sadly.

There was a cosy informality about dinner. Nobody changed, there was too much talking and laughing to be done. Cathy helped Melissa prepare the meal and Dan disappeared with Dave into the study to talk business. The evening passed just as quickly as the afternoon, with delicious food and plenty of wine and laughter.

'When is your baby due?' Dan asked, smiling at Melissa.

'February. Isn't it about time you started a family, Daniel? You're not getting any younger,' she teased in reply.

Cathy flushed as Dan's eyes met hers. His were dark and very serious and she looked away.

'I want Cathy to myself for a while longer,' he drawled easily and very convincingly.

'Lucky Cathy,' Melissa retorted, slipping her arm in Dave's and smiling at Cathy, who could not for the life of her smile back. She felt too shaken by the expression in Dan's eyes in that unguarded moment, even though she had been unable to read it. Did Dan want children? She wanted his children, more than anything in the world.

Soon it was late and time to go to bed. Dan fetched Cathy's forgotten case from the car. 'I'd forgotten, I brought a dress for dinner,' she said to Melissa as they climbed the stairs.

'We don't usually bother, not with friends,' Melissa replied warmly.

'It's a lovely house and Dave's a lovely man— you're very lucky,' Cathy said impulsively, on a small sigh.

'Yes, I am.' Melissa's face was content. 'And so are you. Here's your room. I hope you'll be comfortable, and if there's anything you want, ask. Use the place as your own.'

'Thank you,' smiled Cathy.

The room they entered was long and bright, one wall an enormous window. The walls were white, the carpet deep chocolate brown, the bed an enormous modern four-poster in pine, covered with a snow-white duvet. Cathy looked round at the plants and the African carvings with delight. The room was stark and modern and very comfortable. She washed in the adjoining bathroom, reflecting on what a pleasant evening it had been. She had not felt so happy and relaxed since before moving back with Dan. Back in the bedroom, she began to undress, pulling her nightdress from the overnight case. About to undo her bra, she froze, as Dan, without knocking, strolled into the room, his eyes skimming slowly over her half-naked body.

'What ... what do you want?' she faltered, cheeks burning with embarrassment.

'Sleep,' he replied laconically, pulling open his shirt with tired grace, not looking at her.

Cathy stared at his powerful brown chest, her heart pounding with desire, as he shrugged out of the shirt, the light gleaming on his smooth, wide shoulders.

'What's wrong with your room?' she asked shortly.

Dan lifted his dark brows. 'This is my room,' he replied, his voice expressionless.

'It ... it can't be ... I ... this is my room. . . .' she stammered in confusion.

He sighed impatiently and raked his fingers through his hair. 'Our room,' he corrected. 'Mel and Dave assume that our marriage is fairly normal. There's one room, one double bed for us both to share.' He was being patient, and Cathy felt her teeth grinding together.

'I can't——' she began.

'Go and tell Melissa that. Ask her for another room,' he cut in irritably, and disappeared into the bathroom. As soon as she heard the shower running, Cathy slipped off her underwear and pulled on her nightdress. For some ridiculous reason she had assumed they would be given separate rooms. There was no reason for that assumption, except that they had separate rooms at the apartment and she automatically expected it. How stupid she was! If she had thought about it at all, she would have realised that wherever they stayed they would be treated as an ordinary married couple. It was too late now, she would have to share the room with Dan, her only alternative being an embarrassing explanation to Melissa and a lot of fuss. It was only one night, she thought, trying to make the best of it.

She was sitting in bed when he came back into the room, her head bowed, vulnerable.

'Decided to make the best of it?' he enquired, his voice heavy with sarcasm, reading her mind.

'I hate this pretence,' she said vehemently, feeling hurt.

'So do I.' Dan sounded weary.

'You'll have to sleep on the floor,' she told him, not realising how sharp her voice sounded, only knowing that she could not share a bed with him.

'No way,' Dan drawled coldly. 'There's plenty of room in that bed, there's no need for either of us to sleep on the floor. Goddammit, Cathy, I'm not going to rape you!'

She flinched from the ice in his voice. 'I didn't mean. . . .'

'No?' He didn't believe her. 'You have my word that I won't lay a finger on you. Okay? So you can stop that nasty little mind of yours dead in its tracks.' He made himself very clear and, ridiculously, Cathy felt piqued and frustrated.

She lay down on her side of the bed, turning away from him, stiff and tense and suddenly very cold. He was right, she realised, the bed was big enough for five people, let alone two. It would be silly for one of them to sleep on the floor. Seconds later she felt the mattress give as Dan slid in beside her. She did not realise that she was holding her breath until her lungs became so tight that she had to release it, on a long, shaky sigh.

Dan heard that sigh and shifted restlessly, next to her. 'Relax,' he murmured quietly. 'You're quite safe with me, Cathy. We've been living under the same roof for over two weeks, if I had any intention of jumping on you, I've had plenty of opportunity before now.'

She did not answer, miserable to find that she was crying, her whole body shivering with cold and anguish, torn between anger at his coldness and longing for his warmth, betraying her. 'Cathy—' He groaned her name, reaching for her in the darkness, and pulled her back against the hard warm curve of his body, his arm coiling around her narrow waist. 'God, you're freezing,' he muttered against her hair.

'I'm sorry,' she sobbed, unable to hide her tears any longer. He turned her in his arms then, so that she faced him, staring down at her in the darkness, his hands smoothing back her hair from her wet face.

'Why are you crying? Look, if it's that important to you, I'll sleep on the floor—God knows, I've slept in worse places.' His voice was gentle, teasing, and he framed her face with his hands and wiped away her tears with his thumbs.

'N ... no, stay with me,' she hiccoughed, her hand touching his bare shoulder.

'Why are you so unhappy?' Dan asked wearily, his voice tinged with despair. 'I thought—oh, what the hell! Do you want to leave the apartment, go back to Brighton?'

He was offering to free her again, but she did not want her freedom any more. It was a shock to realise that she had felt more alive in the past fortnight than she had done in the past year. She loved him, and at that moment, as she lay in his arms in the darkness, she accepted his terms, willing to pay any price to be with him. She would not even think about his offer, not now. She was in his arms, and that was so good that she wanted to concentrate on it, lose herself in it.

'I don't want to talk about it,' she whispered desperately. 'Not tonight—I'm too tired. Just hold me, Dan.'

'It's all right. Go to sleep now,' he said softly, hearing the pleading note in her voice, and stroked her hair again, the slow soothing brush of his hand making her eyelids droop as she pressed her face to his chest. His heartbeat thundered in her ears. It was too fast, she thought, vaguely. It was—The thought was never completed, because she was suddenly fast asleep.

CHAPTER TEN

SHE woke early the next morning, feeling refreshed, which made a change, because lately she had been sleeping badly, feeling dreadful when she woke. Not remembering where she was for a second, she stretched her body languorously, freezing into stillness as her limbs came into contact with Dan's.

She opened her eyes warily, remembering the night before, the bright morning light making her blink. She was lying against his body and he was asleep, still holding her with one arm, the other flung out across the bed. She looked up into his face, at the rough growth that shadowed his chin, at the dark hollows beneath his cheekbones and at his warm, sensual mouth, and smiled to herself, tender with love for him. It would be a long time, maybe forever, before she awoke in his bed again, and she wanted to capture the moments so that she could remember them. She touched the hair that matted his chest, it was springy and rough beneath her fingertips. There was a fierce, hungry madness in her blood and she wanted him badly, her fingers stroking lower to the hard flat muscles of his stomach.

Dan's eyes snapped open suddenly, his hand capturing hers, trapping it against his smooth skin. 'What the hell are you playing at?' he demanded huskily.

'Touching you,' she smiled into his brilliant green eyes.

'And I promised not to touch you—you're making it bloody impossible for me to keep that promise,' he muttered roughly.

'Perhaps I don't want you to keep it. Perhaps I want you to make love to me.'

She was beautiful, alluring, impossible to resist. She pulled her hand free and sat up, her eyes inviting as she gracefully pulled off her nightdress. She heard Dan draw breath sharply, unevenly, his eyes glittering as they rested on the warm white swell of her breasts. She leaned over him and kissed his mouth, laughing softly as he reached for her, pulling her against his body and kissing her deeply, hungrily.

He was shaking as he touched her, murmuring

words that she could not understand against her white skin. It was as though they had never been apart. She let her hands stroke over his body, making him groan, shaping the tense, clenched muscles of his back, his shoulders, kissing him sweetly, matching his hunger with a need that blocked out all coherent thought.

She felt the roughness of his thigh parting hers, the erotic warmth of his mouth against her swollen breasts and the softness of her stomach, moaning with pleasure, her hands clenching against his back, her nails raking the smooth tanned skin. Their bodies came together with a wildness, a searing heat. Dan's powerful arms were cruel, his heavy body fierce with a hard, driving energy that demanded total surrender.

Cathy clung to him, lost beneath the sweetness and the urgency of his expert lovemaking, until everything exploded, tearing her apart, shattering her into a million tiny pieces of pure sensation; the tension broke in Dan at the same moment, his hard groan shivering through her. Exhausted, her grip on him finally relaxed and she stared down at his dark head bent to her shoulder, feeling his racing heart striking against her body. She stroked his hair, threading her fingers through the thick vitality of it, her breath finally slowing a little, cold sanity finally invading her mind and making her hot with shame as she realised what she had done.

She had practically begged him to make love to her, taunting him beyond control, after forcing a promise out of him that he would not touch her. It was cruel and contrary and stupid. He would know for sure now how she loved him, she had given herself away completely.

Dan kissed her shoulders, her throat, his mouth

warm and beautiful. He moved so that he lay beside her, still breathing deeply. His eyes were dark, glazed with satisfaction as he smiled at her.

'I've been waiting for you so many nights, wanting you, aching to touch you again,' he murmured, his voice low, drained. He tried to take her into his arms, but she moved, lightning fast, embarrassed colour staining her face, an empty misery engulfing her.

Dan laughed tenderly. 'You're shy!'

'No,' she said painfully, struggling out of bed and pulling on her discarded nightdress. 'Ashamed.'

Dan frowned, jacknifing into a sitting position. 'Ashamed? Why? It was beautiful—you were beautiful.' His warm voice shuddered through her and she let her hair fall in a protective curtain over her flushed face.

That one moment of madness had changed everything. She could not stay with him now, she would have to take the freedom he had offered. Without telling him, though—one look in his eyes told her that as far as he was concerned, the offer was now withdrawn. She was no longer the awkward, unco-operative wife, she was willing, more than willing, if this morning was anything to go by, to be his lover when Natalie Benjamin was not there. It was very convenient for him, she thought bitterly.

'God, I hate you,' she said slowly and clearly.

Dan's face tightened, his mouth hard. 'You wanted me. That's not hate,' he drawled icily.

Regretting her words, words that were totally untrue and only calculated to hurt and anger, not even knowing what had driven her to say them,

Cathy jumped off the bed and ran to the bathroom, locking the door behind her. She heard Dan crashing about in the bedroom, swearing violently, then the slam of the door that told her he had gone.

She felt like crying, but her tears would not come and she knew now why she had spoken to him so cruelly. It was jealousy, sheer blinding jealousy, that her husband, her lover, also gave to another woman the pleasure he gave to her. Damn him!

She showered and dressed, then, plucking up all her courage, went downstairs. There was no sign of Dan, but Melissa was in the kitchen preparing breakfast and judging from her smiling greeting, had no idea that anything was wrong.

They left soon after lunch, Dan apologising, using business as an excuse, and Melissa promising to telephone Cathy to arrange lunch in town the following week. Dan was completely silent all the way back to London, his anger almost tangible in the small confines of the car.

As soon as they got back to the apartment, Cathy went straight to her room, anxious to get out of his way, her nerves almost at breaking point. She heard him leave again within five minutes. He was probably on his way to see Natalie, she thought spitefully. Natalie, who would be only too pleased to soothe his dented ego. The idea came to her in a flash of inspiration. It was the perfect time to leave. If Dan had gone to Natalie, as he surely had, he would be away for some hours.

She quickly packed some essentials, not wanting to carry anything unnecessary, and thought of Joe. She had to get away. Dan had paid Joe's debts and Joe was repaying the loan, so she did not have to

worry about that any more. There was nothing
harmful Dan could do to Joe, now, he was keeping
his side of the bargain. She did not know why she
had not realised that before. If she left, nothing
would change. Dan could take her to court, she
supposed, over the legal agreement she had signed,
but she did not care. She shook her head in amazement. She could have left any time before now.
She was in love with him, though, perhaps she had
hoped he would come to love her in return, if she
stayed long enough. She flayed herself merci-
lessly—so stupid, so honourable, she probably
deserved everything she got. Playing the game by
the rules got you precisely nowhere. Dan had
taught her that, and she had finally learned her
difficult lesson.

She drank a cup of coffee, smoked a cigarette
and wondered where to go. She could not go
directly to her cottage because if, and it was a very
big if, Dan cared to look for her, that would be the
first place he would look. A hotel seemed the only
answer for a few days at least.

She put on her coat and picked up her case,
moving mechanically, her thoughts miles away, and
left the flat for the last time. Then she drove to a
hotel and checked in, only feeling safe when she
was inside her room with the door firmly locked.

Two days later Cathy decided that it was time to
go back to her cottage. If Dan had looked for her
when he found her gone, he would have checked
there immediately. She would be safe there for a
while and it would give her time to decide what on
earth she was going to do with the mess of her
life.

She drove down to Brighton early and had lunch

in a hotel on the sea front, strangely reluctant to go home. That afternoon she walked for miles along the coast and it was late evening before she finally parked her car outside the cottage. She pulled her case out of the trunk and let herself in, locking the front door behind her. She would light the fire, that was her first priority, the place was freezing, then make coffee. She might even feel like a normal human being after that. She pushed open the sitting room door, then fainted dead away at what she saw within.

She returned to consciousness moments later, to find herself lying on the couch, Dan standing over her, his eyes dark with concern. She tried to struggle into a sitting position, but his hands gently pushed her back against the soft velvet cushions.

'Lie still for a moment,' he smiled. Cathy closed her eyes and opened them again. It was no dream. Dan was actually here, in her sitting room. The lights were dim, the fire lit, warming the room, and he was here.

'What are you doing here?' she demanded un-steadily.

He stared down at her, his mouth twisting wryly. 'I've asked myself that same question over and over again. You always run, I always follow—a fact of life, I guess.'

He was being too cryptic. She did not unders-tand. 'Could I have some coffee?' she asked, child-like in the request. Nothing he said made any sense to her, she should be quite resigned to it by now.

'Of course.'

He left the room and she sat up, feeling fine. What on earth was he doing here? How did he get in? Dan returned within minutes handing her a cup of steaming coffee.

'How do you feel?'

'Not bad. Shocked mainly.' She sipped the reviving coffee and stared at him, hungrily. He looked tense, strained, rather tired, but his attraction reached out to her, holding her spellbound as always.

'I've been out of my mind! Where the hell have you been?' he asked very softly, lighting a cigarette.

'A hotel—Dan, why are you here? How did you get in? Where's Natalie?' The questions tumbled out, and she was still too bemused to be thinking clearly.

'I forced the door,' he admitted without remorse. 'I've fixed it, though, so you needn't worry. I came here to find you—and what the hell has Natalie to do with all this?'

'How long have you been here?' she asked, wishing that she had not mentioned Natalie.

'Two days. I guessed that you would come back here in the end, so I waited. I've missed you, Cathy.'

His voice was a cool caress and she lowered her head, colouring brightly. She had missed him too, very badly, but she could not tell him so, silence bound her, as usual. But suddenly she felt defiant. Why should she avoid mentioning Natalie? It was the end for her and Dan, it did not matter any more. A thought struck her. Had Natalie been here, to her cottage? She could not believe that Dan would do that, but she had to know for sure.

'Has Natalie been here?' she demanded.

Dan swore under his breath. 'What is this obsession with Natalie?'

'Has she?'

'Of course she hasn't, why the hell should she come here?' He was angry, the green eyes flashing warning at her—a warning she ignored.

'Why do you lie to me?' she whispered sadly.

'I've never lied to you. Never,' he emphasised coolly.

'Where's Natalie now?'

Dan sighed heavily, humouring her. 'Larry has taken her back to L.A. I think she's on the verge of a breakdown, she still hasn't completely re-covered from Owen's death.' he laughed sourly. 'You wouldn't believe it. Everything is grinding to a halt over there. I tried to reach Raoul on the phone. He was at the hospital, and you can bet your life there'll be no work forthcoming from him until all this is over. The company could go to the wall before he notices.' He was staring into her pale face with an absorbed intensity, hardly aware of what he was saying.

Cathy frowned. 'Raoul? What has he to do with this?'

'Natalie and Raoul,' he replied vaguely, his eyes on her gentle mouth.

'Dan!' She shook his arm urgently, needing to know. There was something beautifully wrong, but she fiercely controlled the tiny spark of hope inside herself. 'Dan, you must tell me everything—*everything* about Natalie and Raoul,' she said desper-ately.

'Cathy. . . .'

'Please, Dan, it's so very important, please!'

'Okay.' He was frowning heavily, staring at her as though she was insane. 'Raoul is crazy about Natalie, he has been for years. She'll have nothing to do with him and it's breaking him up.'

'She wants you,' Cathy said softly.

'I can't help that—she knows damned well that I'm not on offer,' he said harshly.

'Did you send Dick abroad?' Her heart felt as though it was about to burst, but she was controlling herself with a will-power she had never known she possessed.

'Yes.' He was brief, impatient.

'Why?'

'He was the only man for the job. Their marriage was on the rocks even then, he asked for the post and I'm glad I gave it to him. He's working brilliantly out there, pulling in millions in contracts.' He paused. 'Why all your interest in the family history?'

Cathy looked him straight in the eye. 'The day I went shopping with Natalie, the day Owen was taken ill, she told me things. . . .' Her voice broke weakly.

'Tell me,' Dan demanded, suddenly still, intent.

'She . . . she told me that you and she had been lovers for years, that you couldn't marry because Dick wouldn't give her a divorce and because she and her family were Catholic and because Owen's health would suffer. She said it would kill him. She also said that you'd only married me to cover up the affair and to divert gossip and scandal which could be damaging to the company and to the family.'

'And you believed her?' His green eyes were dark, violent, his voice very flat.

Cathy winced. 'Part of me did,' she admitted honestly. 'Before we got married, I was filled with doubts. I couldn't believe that a man like you could possibly want an ordinary nothing-special eighteen-year-old as your wife. I thought I had nothing you could possibly want. I was too withdrawn to talk to anybody about it, it just grew and grew. I was young and so unsure of myself. I asked Raoul, but he was embarrassed, refusing to talk about Natalie, and I'm afraid ... I'm afraid I assumed that he knew about the affair and was being loyal to you. That evening I saw Natalie in your arms in the car. Everything was piling up on top of me and it seemed the final proof, somehow. My pride wouldn't allow me to be used as a diversion for gossip. I heard you and Raoul talking about Dick—it reinforced what Natalie had said, that you'd got rid of him so that you could have her for yourself. She seemed very truthful, very straight— and yes, I believed her. When Owen was taken ill, I knew that her story about his weak heart was also true. It followed, I thought, that the rest of what she'd said....' She could not carry on, the memories were still too raw.

Dan, who had been so silent while she spoke suddenly took her shoulders and turned her to face him. 'Cathy, you have to believe me, I've never touched Natalie, never wanted her. Sure, she made her feelings clear, but I made mine equally clear, right from the start. As far as I'm concerned she is my cousin and she works for me.' His face hardened. 'Although after this, she's out, as fast as I can get rid of her. As for her being in my arms, I don't remember. She was upset about Owen, I may have comforted her, nothing more. I was too damned worried about you at the time. Why the hell didn't you tell me what she'd said?' He was angry, but he was begging for her belief and as everything fell into place, Cathy did believe him. It was all explained so easily, so obviously. She had wrecked her marriage, killed whatever affection

Dan had held for her, because she had been young and stupid and very unsure of herself. It was the biggest mistake of her life and she would have to pay for ever.

She took a deep breath, her eyes shamed. 'I didn't tell you because I believed her. I thought everybody knew but me. It would have been pointless and humiliating, it would have changed nothing and you would have known my jealousy, that I loved you. I still love you, Dan, more than I believed it was possible to love anybody.' She had finally told him, now, when it was too late.

Dan was perfectly still, searching her face, and she lifted her eyes to his, letting her love shine in them. A second later his mouth parted hers, his kiss fierce, almost desperate. 'I love you, Cathy— God, how I love you! Ever since the first moment I saw you at that party, I knew that I'd have you, that I'd never let you go.'

Cathy could hardly believe it was happening, her dream of so long, that Dan would one day love her, was true. She saw it in his eyes, his face, in the tension of his body. 'But you let me go,' she whispered, softly touching his face.

'I had to,' he groaned, his mouth moving against her hair. 'I had no other choice, even though I felt as though you'd stuck a knife in my ribs. You were young, so very young, and I knew I was too old for you, but I couldn't let go. I'm not proud of the way I rushed you into marriage, but I was beyond reason even then, obsessed with the thought of possessing you, keeping you. I swore to myself that if you ever wanted to go, I'd have to set you free.' He sighed heavily. 'I knew that you couldn't feel as deeply as I did and I couldn't force that sort of responsibility on you. When you came to me that day, I was sure that I'd frightened you away. I had to let you go, do you understand?'

His voice was tormented, rough with emotion. 'I could have killed you, so easily, when you told me about that other man. It was a dangerous, violent jealousy, I had to get away, let you get away before I hurt you. And the private detective. . . .' He shrugged, his mouth compressing wryly. 'More jealousy. I had to know who he was and I had to know that you were safe. There was no other man, and I was forced to admit to myself that I'd frightened you away, forced to admit that you didn't love me. I'm sorry, Cathy, it was a dirty trick, but I was at my wits' end, it was the worst time I can remember.' He smiled. 'Larry was sick of seeing me, sick of hearing my troubles.'

Cathy kissed his brown throat. 'I thought you went to Natalie for comfort,' she teased softly, desperately happy that he hadn't.

'That bitch, she tried so damned hard!'

'She's ill,' Cathy reminded him gently.

'That's bloody obvious,' Dan said roughly. Then he smiled. 'I'm sorry.' Cathy smiled back at him. 'You warned her off last week,' she remembered.

'Yes, I didn't want her upsetting you,' he admitted simply.

'I'm glad that you found out there was nobody else. I regretted those lies so much, but it seemed the only way to make you free me. I would have been destroyed if I'd stayed, loving you as I do.'

'Cathy.' He kissed her again, slowly, deeply, his warm mouth lingering hungrily.

'Why did you send Joe away?' she asked against his mouth. It seemed vitally important that everything should be straightened out between them before they started again. A new life, a second chance—the very thought filled her with happiness.

'I'd been keeping my eye on you, waiting and waiting for another chance with you, and when you came to my office, I thought my prayers were answered. It was my chance and I grabbed it ruthlessly. But sending Joe to L.A. had nothing to do with that. I did it because I knew it would be good for him, to make it on his own, and good for you—you were out of your mind with worry. He was using you, and I wanted to put an end to that.'

'You were right, and it's worked very well,' she admitted.

'I know.' Dan smiled at her wickedly. 'I knew you were seeing Calvert and I was as mad as hell about it. I had to get rid of him, he wanted you nearly as much as I did and you were being kind to him. So I made up that story about needing a wife, and it seemed perfect. It got rid of Calvert, it didn't frighten you and it was also a shield for my feelings. I was determined not to blow it again. That's why I promised not to touch you, I thought you'd hate me if we made love. It seemed true at Mel and Dave's.' He was unrepentant, but she saw the flicker of pain in his eyes.

'When we made love, I thought you knew that I loved you, I was afraid because I was sure you didn't love me. I'm sorry I was so nasty.' She kissed him, then smiled. 'You were terribly rude to Greg.'

'I was crazy with jealousy, you were so miserable to see him go.'

'He was a good friend, and I had no idea how he felt. He knew that I loved you, he always knew that. I was sad to hurt him—that's all, honestly!' she added laughingly, as she saw his jaw clenching. 'Dan, we've made so many mistakes, me in particular. Can you forgive me? Can we start again?' They were the most important questions she had ever asked, and she held her breath waiting for his answer.

'I'm not letting you go, Cathy, not again. We'll make it this time, because there's nothing but the truth between us. We have a lifetime ahead of us.' He kissed her briefly, hungrily. 'And what do you mean forgive, you crazy child? There's nothing to forgive, there never will be,' he said firmly.

'When we're in England, will we live in that beautiful house?' she asked beggingly.

'The one that you won't decorate?' he teased. 'Yes, I bought it for you. It was strange, I knew as soon as I saw it.'

'So did I,' Cathy agreed, her voice suddenly trembling as he began to undo her blouse, his strong hands sure and unhurried and arousing. He undressed her, his eyes glittering with a fevered desire as he stared at her body.

'I love you, Cathy,' he murmured deeply. 'I need you.'

She reached for him, her arms sliding around his neck to pull him closer. 'Dan my love,' she whispered his name achingly. He found her mouth slowly, his touch was fire and he was everything she would ever want. As they made love the knowledge that they had nearly lost each other brought them together desperately. At last admitted, one love that could not be touched and could never be broken.

THE PLACE FOR WHAT AILS YOU

In 1750, an English physician named Dr. Richard Russell prescribed "sea-bathing" as a cure for a variety of illnesses. Little did he know that his prescription would start a fashion: it wasn't long before flocks of English aristocrats headed for the beaches of a sleepy fishing village called Brighthelmstone, fifty miles south of London, to put Dr. Russell's remedy into action.

Soon Brighthelmstone became better known as Brighton, our heroine's hometown and today a well-known resort on the shores of the English Channel. In 1783, the Prince of Wales, who was later to become King George IV, followed the trend set by other aristocrats. He fell so in love with the beaches of Brighton that he built his own palace, the Royal Pavilion, there. Probably the most exotic royal residence in Europe, it was designed in the style of the Mogul palaces of India, complete with elaborate mosaics and minarets. By 1822, Brighton had been transformed from a fishing village to an elegant resort of Regency mansions with creamy white facades, long terraces, bay windows and balconies overlooking proper English gardens.

Today, Brighton is still popular—except that visitors now bathe in the sea for fun rather than for health. The Royal Pavilion has become a museum, and many of the Regency mansions are hotels.

The modern tourist will also be delighted by the discovery of The Lanes, a quaint little neighborhood of streets so narrow that no automobile can pass through, and lined with antique shops, boutiques and cafés. The Lanes is none other than the huddle of fishermen's cottages once called Brighthelmstone—and it is still considered the heart of Brighton even as it was before sea-bathing became a fashion.

Legacy of
PASSION

BY CATHERINE KAY

A love story begun long ago comes full circle...

Venice, 1819: Contessa Allegra di Rienzi, young, innocent, unhappily married. She gave her love to Lord Byron—scandalous, irresistible English poet. Their brief, tempestuous affair left her with a shattered heart, a few poignant mementos—and a daughter he never knew about.

Boston, today: Allegra Brent, modern, independent, restless. She learned the secret of her great-great-great-grandmother and journeyed to Venice to find the di Rienzi heirs. There she met the handsome, cynical, blood-stirring Conte Renaldo di Rienzi, and like her ancestor before her, recklessly, hopelessly lost her heart.

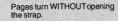

SUPERROMANCE

Longer, exciting, sensuous and dramatic!

Fascinating love stories that will hold
you in their magical spell till the last page
is turned!

Now's your chance to discover the earlier
books in this exciting series. Choose from
the great selection on the following page!

SUPERROMANCE

Complete and mail this coupon today!

Worldwide Reader Service

In the U.S.A.
1440 South Priest Drive
Tempe, AZ 85281

In Canada
649 Ontario Street
Stratford, Ontario N5A 6W2

Please send me the following SUPERROMANCES. I am enclosing my check or money order for $2.50 for each copy ordered, plus 75¢ to cover postage and handling.

☐ # 8   ☐ # 14   ☐ # 20
☐ # 9   ☐ # 15   ☐ # 21
☐ # 10   ☐ # 16   ☐ # 22
☐ # 11   ☐ # 17   ☐ # 23
☐ # 12   ☐ # 18   ☐ # 24
☐ # 13   ☐ # 19   ☐ # 25

Number of copies checked @ $2.50 each = $_____
N.Y. and Ariz. residents add appropriate sales tax $_____
Postage and handling $_____.75
TOTAL $_____

I enclose _____ .
(Please send check or money order. We cannot be responsible for cash sent through the mail.)
Prices subject to change without notice.

NAME_____
(Please Print)
ADDRESS_____APT. NO._____
CITY_____
STATE/PROV._____
ZIP/POSTAL CODE_____

Offer expires August 31, 1983   30256000000